The carriage had gone halfway around the park when Stewart broke the silence between them and squeezed her hand.

"I'm glad you came with me to Manhattan. I've wanted to speak to you before now, but it never seemed like the right opportunity. You see, I've come to care a great deal for you, Myra. . . ."

His words sent a shaft of bittersweet pain slicing through her, and she laid trembling fingers over his mouth. "Please, Stewart. Don't do this."

"I love you, Myra," he said, his warm breath fanning over her fingers and sending tiny little shivers through her.

"You can't love me," she argued, a catch in her voice as he pulled her hand away and lowered his head toward her.

"It's too late for that."

When his lips touched hers, she didn't resist. Soon he would be out of her life for good, and that knowledge spurred her to wrap her arms around his neck and return his kiss with fervor. He stiffened momentarily, then drew her closer. After a moment he lifted his head, his eyes anguished.

"You're crying!" he exclaimed softly. "Why are you crying?"

She shook her head, wiping the tears away with an unsteady hand.

"Myra. . .?"

She studied his strong features, his soft hazel eyes, his firm, sensitive mouth, knowing it was the last time she'd ever do so. He'd shown her gentleness, consideration, and he had helped her find her way to God. And he'd taught her the true meaning of love. She would miss him dearly.

PAMELA GRIFFIN lives in Texas and divides her time between family, church activities, and writing. She fully gave her life to the Lord Jesus Christ in 1988, after a rebellious young adulthood, and owes the fact that she's still alive today to an all-loving and forgiving God and to a mother who steadfastly prayed and had faith that God could bring her wayward daughter "home." Pamela's main goal in writing Christian romance is to help and encourage those who do know the Lord and to plant a seed of hope in those who don't. Pamela invites you to check out her website: http://home.att.net/~words_of_honey/Pamela.htm.

Books by Pamela Griffin

HEARTSONG PRESENTS
HP372—'Til We Meet Again

In the Secret Place

Pamela Griffin

Heartsong Presents

To all those searching for peace: He holds the key.

Much thanks to my critique partners on this project: Tamela H.M., Donita T., and Mom. Also thanks to Tracey B., Paige W. D., Lianne L., Lena D., and Francie for their helpful suggestions.

And to my Lord and Savior, Jesus Christ, who rescued me from the miry pit and set my feet upon the solid Rock. Thank you for loving me when I was unlovable and for never giving up on me.

A note from the author:
I love to hear from my readers! You may correspond with me by writing:
Pamela Griffin
Author Relations
PO Box 719
Uhrichsville, OH 44683

ISBN 1-58660-167-9

IN THE SECRET PLACE

Cover illustration by Lorraine Bush.

prologue

April 14, 1912

Charlotte braced trembling hands on the carpet. Pain shot through her wrist as she slowly pushed herself to a standing position and drew her wrapper tight. This was the worst Eric had ever treated her. Had no one heard what happened? Why hadn't a steward come to investigate the crash when Eric swiped her personal items off the dresser or threw a chair against the wall?

She looked in the mirror at her pale, battered face. Her lower lip was swollen and bleeding, an eye was blackened, and a trickle of blood dripped from her nose. She dipped a cloth in the pitcher of lukewarm water beside the bed. Wincing, she dabbed at the damaged skin. How could her body throb with such pain while at the same time she felt so empty inside?

She scanned the mess on the floor with dulled eyes. The glow from the gaslight reflected off a cylindrical object that had rolled partway underneath the dresser. She recognized it as the bottle with the drug Eric had forced her to use on Edward Mooreland.

She dropped to her knees and grabbed it up, bringing it to her chest, as though it were something dearly cherished. There was enough left to provide a lethal dose, she was certain. She had only put a pinch into Edward's drink to make him forgetful, and the vial was still full.

Her hand shaking, Charlotte poured water from the pitcher into a tumbler and added the entire contents of the small bottle, turning it upside down and clinking it against the lip of the glass until not one bit of the white powder remained.

Nobody wanted her. Eric didn't love her. And his shocking

5

revelation as he had sneered down at her before slamming out of her stateroom sent stabs of pain through her heart—a heart that she hadn't thought could feel any more pain after her three-year association with Eric.

She'd been wrong.

God certainly couldn't care for a person like her, no matter what Annabelle and Myra said to the contrary. Charlotte was alone. Desperately alone. And it would always be that way. She would always live under the threat of Eric's wrath, always have to endure the abuse that came more often than it used to, always bear the sorrow of her mother's sin. . .unless she put a stop to it right now.

Holding the glass between her hands, she looked down, several tears falling into the murky liquid. "God," she said in a wobbly voice, "if only what Annabelle had said was true. If only You could have loved me—in spite of what I am, what I've become. Maybe. . .maybe my life would have been different then."

Closing her eyes, Charlotte gave a strangled sob and raised the glass to her throbbing lips.

The ship gave a sudden jolt. Crystal teardrops hanging from the gaslight jarred together with a discordant clink. Already shaky, Charlotte lost her balance and fell forward, losing her grip on the tumbler. The liquid splashed onto the cream-colored carpet. Staring at the dark spot in angry frustration, she curled up into a ball and began to cry.

❧

The sound of frantic knocking penetrated her mind.

Charlotte sat up and wiped her eyes. Again the rapid knock came—louder this time. She thought about ignoring it, then changed her mind and shuffled to the door. The sight of fellow passenger Annabelle Mooreland shocked Charlotte—probably as much as Charlotte's own appearance shocked Annabelle.

The brunette stared, wide-eyed. "What happened to you, Charlotte? Who did this to you?"

"It–it's nothing. I ran into a door. A foolish mistake." Even as she said the words, Charlotte knew the explanation sounded ridiculous. But she couldn't tell the truth.

Annabelle's expression conveyed disbelief, yet she didn't pursue the matter. "The captain has asked all passengers to take their life belts and go to the boat deck. The steward says it's nothing to be concerned about—merely a precaution. I–I just wanted you to know."

"Thank you, Miss Mooreland. It was kind of you to tell me." Charlotte swallowed hard. She desperately wanted to tell Annabelle how sorry she was and to confess her part in Annabelle's loss. It was partly due to her that Annabelle no longer had a home to go to upon reaching America and that she had lost her mother's diamond jewelry—though she probably hadn't yet discovered that. Eric had been quite clever. But Charlotte could never say anything to the young woman.

Suddenly Charlotte felt old, though she'd only turned twenty a month ago. "Thank you," she murmured a second time before closing the door with a soft click.

She dressed, her bruised body complaining with every movement. Noticing the life belt stowed on the high shelf in the closet, she gave it one wry glance before turning away.

On the boat deck, Charlotte saw Myra Flannigan, a young lady she'd met on the second-class promenade when she'd sought escape from Eric's black moods. Myra was traveling to America to live with an uncle whom she'd never seen, her mother having recently died. Charlotte had struck up a tentative acquaintance with the young woman, but now hastened back to the companionway before Myra could see her, embarrassed by her ravaged appearance.

A steward saw her, his eyes widening, and asked if she was all right. Charlotte gave him the same explanation she'd given Annabelle and hurried away.

A flicker of hope lit within her, a half-formed idea begging for release. What if all were not lost? What if she could redeem herself in some way? Make up for a small portion of the evil activities in which she'd been involved these past three years?

The flame of hope fanned into a blaze of excitement, giving her renewed energy, and she returned to her deck, passing her room and continuing on to Eric's adjoining cabin. Remembering the fury she'd endured at his hands, she hesitated, bit her lip, and then knocked softly. When no one answered, she pushed the door open.

The room was empty.

She clutched the door frame, almost passing out from relief, then hurried to his trunk. Shoulders and back protesting the strain, she lifted the heavy lid, wincing as a twinge of pain shot through her wrist. She rifled through the interior until she found what she was looking for. Smiling through her pain, she stuffed the items into her deep coat pocket and hurried out the door, hoping she wouldn't run into Eric.

As the night progressed, it became obvious that the *Titanic* was sinking due to the iceberg it had struck. With incredible calm, Charlotte moved past frantic throngs of people, looking for one person; but she was unable to locate her. There weren't many lifeboats left. Had Annabelle already departed?

Charlotte furrowed her brow. She'd intended to give Annabelle the things that were rightfully hers—the deed to her house, which Eric had unfairly won in a card game with Annabelle's father, and the diamond jewelry he'd stolen. Charlotte wanted nothing more than to return to her room and let blissful death overtake her. She had nothing to live for. Yet she so wanted to do this one good deed before she died.

"Excuse me, Miss. You must get into the lifeboat!"

Charlotte snapped out of her musings and realized that she stood at the edge of the crowd, in front of one of the wooden boats.

"Oh, but I don't—"

Her denial was interrupted as she was accidentally pushed from behind, the crowd growing more frantic. In a single move, the steward grabbed her before she fell headlong into the boat, which hovered a great distance above the water. Despite her protests, he handed her down to another crewman, who grabbed her arm and practically swung her to a seat. Her bruised body protested the rough treatment. She tried to rise, to give someone else her place, but her legs stubbornly refused to cooperate. Charlotte crumpled, her sobs blending in with those around her. But she was sure her reason for crying wasn't the same as the others'. These women cried for those who'd been left behind. Charlotte cried because she wasn't one of them.

❧

The time in the lifeboat was tedious, bone chilling. Charlotte was lost in another world as she watched the mighty *Titanic* live its last and sink, foot by dreadful foot, below the dark ocean water until it disappeared forever. Another woman passenger held her while tears for all those who had died flowed silently down Charlotte's battered face.

As she looked at the life-jacketed bodies bobbing in the freezing water, Charlotte recognized the still form of her friend Myra Flannigan. Myra's bright copper hair streamed around an alabaster white face. Her eyes, open wide, stared sightlessly at the star-speckled sky. Her head lay at an unusual angle, her neck obviously having been broken when she fell or jumped into the ocean.

Closing her eyes, Charlotte felt a terrible pang of grief at the loss of her sweet friend, who, like Annabelle, had tried to talk to her about God's love. Why had someone as good as Myra been taken while Charlotte was spared?

Amid the many cries piercing the chill night air, Charlotte heard a soft cry for help not far from their lifeboat.

"Someone help her," Charlotte pleaded.

The crewman on the seat in front turned to look at her over his shoulder. "There's no room."

"Then push me over the side and give her my seat."

The man studied her as if she were crazy, and the woman holding Charlotte stroked her tangled hair. "There there, dear," she murmured. She spoke again, addressing the crewman this time. "Poor thing is out of her head. You can't very well blame her, considering all that's happened."

He gave Charlotte one more look, then turned away. Frustrated, she closed her eyes, resigned that for some reason she was meant to live. Tears slipped down her cheeks, unheeded.

When dawn came, they finally were spotted by a ship, the *Carpathia*. The woman next to Charlotte helped position her in a sling used to pull up some of the passengers. Her mind in a fog, Charlotte could barely understand the crewman's words to her as he helped her out of the sling. She had only taken a few steps before a terrible pain racked her middle.

She sank to the wooden planks, everything going black.

☙

Charlotte woke in a dimly lit room, feeling empty and hurting terribly. A doctor, judging from the stethoscope around his neck, came to her side, his brown eyes gentle.

"Shhh—lay back now," he said, putting a smooth hand to her shoulder when she tried to sit up. He sat on the edge of the cot. "Was your husband aboard the *Titanic*, also?"

Swallowing hard, she nodded.

"I'm sorry. Of course, there's a chance he might have made it."

The words did little to reassure Charlotte, having entirely the opposite effect. Was Eric searching for her? What would he do if he found her? Had he discovered her last-minute visit to his cabin?

The doctor looked ill at ease. "I'm afraid I have to tell you that you lost the baby."

Baby? Charlotte closed her eyes and thankfully sank back into deep oblivion.

The next time she awoke, the room was brighter, the sun streaming through a porthole. "Thirsty," she croaked to a blond stewardess sitting nearby.

The woman immediately poured a glass of water and held

it to Charlotte's parched lips. "There, now. Don't drink it too fast—you'll make yourself sick." She pulled the glass away and looked sympathetically down at Charlotte. "We'll likely be reaching America tomorrow. I need your name, Luv, so I can give it to the officer to record on the list of survivors."

Charlotte took a deep breath and, praying God would not strike her dead, clutched the bedcovers at her side.

"Myra Flannigan," she rasped.

one

After the *Carpathia* docked in New York Harbor amid a terrible thunderstorm, Charlotte began to have second thoughts about what she'd done. The idea of taking Myra's identity had come to her during the long hours in the lifeboat.

Myra had told Charlotte that she'd never met her uncle. And both Charlotte and Myra had red hair, green eyes, and similar features, just in case Michael Larkin knew what his niece looked like. Charlotte and Myra came from England, and Charlotte had been surprised to learn they both had lived in London—though on opposite sides of the city. It seemed the perfect plan.

If Eric had survived, he would look for her. And Charlotte could never go back to that kind of life. Never. The one time she'd tried to escape, two months after the wedding ceremony—after Eric had revealed his true nature—he had nearly killed her.

Charlotte put a hand to her throat, remembering the grip of his slim, ironlike fingers. Again she could almost feel the incredible pressure and pain building in her head as his hold maliciously tightened, cutting off her breath; she could almost hear the whispered threats that if she ever left him, he'd hunt her down and kill her, then dispose of her body in the Thames.

Like he'd done with Lord Appleby.

Charlotte shivered and closed her eyes.

A soft knock sounded on the door before a young stewardess popped her head inside. "I just wanted to let you know that the call for second-class passengers to depart should be in about five minutes."

"Thank you." Charlotte managed a smile.

The stewardess shifted, her uneasy gaze straying from Charlotte's face. "The doctor told me to ask if you have anyone to pick you up, Mum. Being as how your husband. . ." Her words trailed away, and she bit her lip.

"Please inform the doctor that someone will be there to greet me. And thank you both for your care these past few days."

"I still think you should go to the hospital, Mum."

Charlotte shook her head, wondering what the fresh-faced stewardess would say if she told her that pain was no stranger to her. "Thank you, no. I would rather go home to recuperate."

The stewardess nodded, her brows drawn together, and closed the door.

Charlotte looked down at her clasped hands. Home? She had no family, no home, no one to care what happened to her—not as Charlotte. She wanted this chance to start over. Surely pretending to be Myra wasn't so terribly wrong.

Charlotte's eyes shifted to the porthole as she remembered snippets of what Myra had told her. Michael was a lonely, childless widower who lived in a peaceful country home. Wouldn't playing the part of his niece and giving him companionship be better than letting the truth be told? Better than forcing him to continue a life of solitude, knowing that his kin was dead? Charlotte would offer him a living niece and in return find sweet refuge, giving her physical and emotional wounds time to heal.

During the past three years, Charlotte had learned the fine art of acting, thanks to Eric's stern tutelage. How many times had she smiled and laughed when her heart was breaking and fear was her closest companion? At least she could retain her British accent, which had been such a hard thing not to do when Eric insisted she play the role of his sister and speak in French, as she had these past weeks.

Yet. . .what if she was caught in the lie? She had never assumed another person's identity before—someone real, that is. Her disguises had always been just that—disguises. Made-up names and identities.

But if Eric was out there looking for Charlotte Fontaneau. . . A chill coursed through her, and she came to a firm decision.

She would do it; she had no other choice.

&

Thunder still shook the air when the second-class passengers were allowed to disembark and walk down the canopied gangplank. At least the storm was passing, the rain not falling as heavily as it had.

On wobbly legs, Charlotte made her way to the street, stumbling amid crying and sorrowful groups of people swarming around her—meeting loved ones, crying over the ones they'd lost. A large area had been roped off for the *Titanic* passengers, to give them privacy from the curious public. Charlotte walked toward the "F" section, where the steward had directed her to go.

Long lines of people stood in the rain under black umbrellas, curiously watching from two blocks away. And the rude reporters had found a place up front, cameras at the ready. Their magnesium flares exploded into the night, rivaling the lightning that illuminated the sky at long intervals.

To Charlotte's shock, several reporters had stood onboard a steamer in a thunderstorm hours earlier, when the *Carpathia* first approached her berth. Charlotte had stood at the porthole, watching and listening as the men shouted questions through a megaphone to the *Titanic* survivors who lined the decks of the *Carpathia*. The reporters offered a high price for an exclusive story, claiming they would catch anyone who wanted to jump aboard their steamer.

Charlotte shook her head at the memory, then suddenly another thought came to her mind as intrusively as the cold rain pelting her face. "F" was the first letter of the surname Flannigan, but it was also the first letter of the name Fontaneau. What if Eric had survived? Could he be here? Was he looking for her even now?

Resisting the impulse to turn and run, she made herself walk to where the "F" passengers and their friends and family congregated. She shook, but not from the cold. Forcing herself to look at the pale and saddened faces from behind the safety of the turned-up collar of her coat, she felt relieved when she didn't spot Eric. But there were so many, and it was hard to tell, as family members rushed to claim their loved ones.

"Papa!"

Tears came to Charlotte's eyes as she watched a blond little girl detach herself from the crowd and run into her father's outstretched arms. He grabbed her around the waist and straightened, pulling her up with him. Holding her tightly against his chest, he bestowed fierce kisses upon her cheek and neck. A pale, slender woman with hair the same color as the child's hurried through the crowd and reached his side. He threw one arm around her, while keeping his hold on his daughter as if he'd never let her go, and kissed the woman soundly on the lips, uncaring of the disapproving looks he received from an elderly matron who stood nearby.

Legs unable to support her any longer, Charlotte leaned against a brick building, then gave in and wearily slid to the wet pavement, unmindful of the few curious stares she received. Tears dripped down her cheeks, mixing with the rain. Why couldn't she have had a father like that? Or a husband who cared? Of course, she knew the reason why.

She'd been conceived in sin, her life going downhill as the years progressed. She didn't deserve happiness. All she hoped for now was peace. Surely that wouldn't be asking too much after all she'd been through. . .would it?

Charlotte wasn't certain how much time passed before she became aware of someone standing in front of her. Opening her eyes, she noted a pair of scuffed men's shoes, shiny from the rain. Her gaze lifted to the long black trousers, up the broad chest covered with a black coat, past the unsmiling mouth to a pair of very concerned eyes under a bowler hat.

Dark hair plastered his forehead.

The man drew in his breath quickly. "What in thunderation happened to you?"

The words were harsh, but the baritone was deep and soft, yet unusual with its clipped accent. He crouched in front of her, and she could see kindness in the golden-green depths of his eyes.

Automatically she lifted a weary hand and touched the bruise under her eye. "It–it was a hard night. . . ."

His dark brows bunched with sympathy. "I understand, Myra—you are Myra Flannigan?" he added, his forehead creasing into a worried frown.

She hesitated only a second, then nodded.

"Your uncle asked me to come and see if you'd survived." With his forefinger and thumb, he pulled the brim of his hat further down over his brow and shifted, obviously uncomfortable. "Nobody's been able to get through with any information over the telegraph, and the White Star Line's offices have been jam-packed for days," he explained. "Michael would have liked to come himself, but I'm afraid the news sent him to his bed. He took the news of the sinking pretty badly."

"Is he ill?" Charlotte asked, alarmed.

"He'll be all right once he knows you're safe. But never mind that now. We have to get you out of this rain and to dry lodgings. Can you walk?" She nodded, and he looked beyond her, as if searching for something. "Have you any luggage?"

"No," she said quietly, her gaze lowering to the street. "Everything went down with the ship."

He blew out a harsh breath. "How thoughtless of me—I should've known. Here, let me help you up, and we'll leave this place. I've booked two rooms at a nearby hotel. Tomorrow morning we'll take the train upstate to your uncle's home."

Charlotte put her small hands into his strong ones, and he

pulled her to her feet. She looked up at him, her eyes widening. He was so tall! She barely came to his shoulder.

His eyes narrowed and a strange look came into them. . . . Suspicion?

Charlotte swallowed hard and began to sway as the wet pavement seemed to move beneath her feet. With lightning speed the stranger reached out and grasped her upper arms, catching her against him. Her knees buckled, and she heard him utter a mild oath before he scooped her up into his arms.

Eyes sliding shut, Charlotte experienced something she'd never known. Security. His arms felt strong and solid.

Like a little child, Charlotte nestled her face against the tweed covering his muscular chest, comforted by the steady thud of his heartbeat and more exhausted than she'd ever been. Before she drifted away, she thought she felt his lips brush the top of her head.

&

"Wake up. We're here."

At the soft-spoken but insistent words, Charlotte forced open heavy eyelids. She sat in a hansom cab with the stranger who'd picked her up from the wharf, her head against his shoulder. Straightening as quickly as she could in her groggy condition, she stared out the rain-streaked pane. They sat in front of a hotel, its lighted windows blazing into the stormy night.

The man alit from the closed carriage, taking his wallet out of an inside coat pocket to pay the driver.

"No, Sir," Charlotte heard the driver say. "This one's on me." When the stranger protested, the driver replied, "I want to do what I can to help those poor souls who was on the *Titanic*."

The stranger offered a quiet thank you, replaced his wallet, and held out a hand to assist Charlotte. Together they rushed through the hotel door—which a uniformed doorman hurriedly opened for them—and into a brightly lit, spacious area. Even in her befuddled state, Charlotte was aware of the luxurious surroundings, crystal chandeliers, and deep pile carpeting. The middle-aged man at the desk glanced up at them. Instantly his aloof expression changed to shock when his dark gaze traveled over Charlotte's face.

"*Titanic?*" he asked as they approached the desk.

The stranger next to her looked taken aback, but nodded. "I've reserved two suites for the night. Name is Stewart Lyons."

"Of course, Mr. Lyons." The manager scanned the open ledger on the polished desk in front of him, then hit the bell at his elbow. A young bellhop in a bright blue uniform with gold braid and a blue pillbox hat instantly appeared.

"Take Mr. Lyons's luggage to rooms 204 and 206," the manager told the freckle-faced boy.

"That won't be necessary," Stewart replied. "We haven't any luggage."

A stunned then sorrowful look flitted across the manager's face before his placid expression returned. "Of course." He handed the bellboy the keys to the rooms, then turned back to Stewart. "I hope you enjoy your stay with us. We want to serve you as our guests. Whatever you need, you have only to ask."

Stewart pulled out his wallet. "I'd like to settle the bill now. We have an early train to catch. . . ."

The manager raised both hands, palms outward. "Please, when I said you are our guests, I meant that in the fullest sense of the word. All rooms and meals are free to *Titanic* passengers."

"In that case I'll pay for my room only. I wasn't on the *Titanic*. I'm here as a friend."

Puzzled, the manager looked from Stewart to Charlotte, but shook his dark head. "No, I insist. You are both our guests."

Resigned, Stewart replaced his wallet, thanked the man, and together he and Charlotte followed the bellboy to the lift.

"Right this way, Sir," the young lad said when the wire cage opened to a long, carpeted hallway. Once they reached room 204, the bellboy unlocked the carved white door and swung it open with a flourish.

Charlotte was vaguely aware of lush furnishings in rose and gold, deep carpeting, and a tapestry settee against one papered wall of cabbage roses. A door on the opposite wall led to what she hoped contained a bed.

"I'll leave you to rest, then," Stewart said softly, his eyes once more scanning her face with concern. "Would you like a bite to eat before you retire?"

Charlotte shook her head, wanting nothing but sleep.

The bellboy, who looked no older than fourteen, gazed up at her, his brown eyes ablaze with the childish light of curiosity. "Were you really on the *Titanic,* Miss?" At Charlotte's hesitant nod, he asked, a thread of excitement in his voice, "What was it like when the ship went down?"

Stewart gave the lad a stern look.

"It was a nightmare," Charlotte replied in a monotone, to which the lad had the grace to look abashed for his impudence. Charlotte managed a tight smile before she closed the door.

★

The next morning Charlotte answered a knock on her door, surprised to see the man who had picked her up from the wharf standing there with a woman's black hat and veil. The headpiece looked as if it had been out of fashion for years.

Clearly embarrassed, he handed it to her. "The maid gave this to me when I asked her where I could buy a hat or scarf for you. It seems they have a receptacle for lost items left behind by former guests. She assured me this has been there for years, so I doubt the former owner will come to claim it."

He shifted and looked away from her face. "I thought you might want something to conceal your condition from curious stares."

"Thank you," she said softly, accepting the hat and wishing she could remember his last name. "Everyone has been so kind."

For the first time he took note of her dress, with the water stain on the front of the skirt, and his brows drew together in a frown. "I should have found you some clothes, as well. I apologize, but there isn't time now. We must hurry to catch the train. I sent a wire to your uncle, telling him to expect us by midday."

Charlotte nodded. "I won't be but a minute." She grabbed her long coat and slipped it on, then pinned the pancake hat over her head and lowered the dark veil over her face, thankful for the anonymity the headpiece provided.

The congested streets hustled with people, even this early in the day. Tall buildings flanked the roads and towered to the rain-washed sky, causing Charlotte to open her eyes wide. Last night she'd seen little of the city, as tired as she had been. Manhattan was cluttered with buildings and very crowded—much like London.

The hired cab left them off at Seventh Avenue at Pennsylvania Station, and she walked close to Stewart as they entered the massive pink granite building with Doric columns running all along its front. Stewart went immediately to the carriages next to the inside entrance and told one of the waiting drivers to take them to the "Penn side." Soon they came to a vast waiting room featuring a vaulted, coffered ceiling with honey-colored stone walls and columns and pink marble floors.

Stewart pulled out his pocket watch. "Our train is due to arrive in ten minutes. We need to hurry."

He took her elbow and increased his pace. Feeling a bit overwhelmed, Charlotte did her best to keep up, and soon they arrived in another large room with a vaulted ceiling made entirely of arched panes of glass. Charlotte felt as if she'd entered a bird cage. Dust motes danced in the sunshine streaming through the sparkling panes and casting pools of light on the stone floors. Almost immediately their train was announced, and Stewart hustled her down the stairs. They waited for passengers to exit the train, then took the few steps up and threaded their way down the narrow aisle until they found an empty compartment. Soon they were on their way, and Charlotte let out a deep sigh of relief.

Stewart, seated opposite her, regarded her with amusement. "Wait till you ride the subway. The rails are underneath the city."

Charlotte looked away from the window and faced him. "Oh?" A lot like the Underground in London, she supposed, though she'd never used that mode of transportation. The thought of going underneath the city frightened her.

"The subway opened in 1904 and is known as the Interborough Rapid Transit," he explained. "Should we ever return, I'll take you there. It's a relatively short trip to Manhattan by train."

"It's kind of you to offer, Mr. . . ." She stopped and gave a rueful shrug. "I'm sorry, I'm afraid I don't remember your name."

He paused a long moment, an unreadable look in his eyes, before he turned his head to stare out the spotted window.

"Lyons," he said, his voice deepening. "Stewart Lyons."

"Thank you, Mr. Lyons."

"Call me Stewart. I'm your uncle's friend, as well as his attorney."

"His attorney?" How ironic. She wondered what he would do if he knew a woman who'd engaged in a life of crime sat across from him. A woman who this very moment carried stolen diamonds and a deed to a stranger's house. She'd likely be booted off the train or perhaps find herself sitting behind bars in a filthy cell.

His gaze snapped her way, an eyebrow lifting at her startled tone. "Does that shock you?"

Charlotte felt her face grow hot. "No—yes. I mean. . ." She searched for something to say. "You seem so young."

She watched as the corner of his mouth turned up into a slow grin. "And is that a bad thing for a lawyer? Being young?"

"Of course not." Her reply was quick. "I thought it took a long time to become a barrister, at least that's what I'd heard.

And—and you don't look old enough to have gone through the years of schooling it must entail. At least it takes a long time to acquire the certificate in England, from what I've heard," she ended miserably.

"Yes, it's the same here in America. And to answer the question you seem so hesitant to ask, I'm twenty-nine years old—going on thirty—and have been a lawyer for three years."

"Oh," she murmured, stunned by his bluntness. Were all Americans so straightforward?

"And," he continued, "if memory serves me correctly, I believe Michael mentioned that you are twenty-one. So young," he teased with a wistful sigh.

She slowly shook her head, furrowing her brow.

The sparkle in his eyes disappeared. "Yet, for being so young, you look as if you carry the weight of the entire world on your shoulders."

Charlotte turned away and stared at the rows of neat, box-like houses the train sped past.

"Did you have friends on the *Titanic*?" he asked.

"Yes," she answered softly, thinking of Annabelle and Myra, and of course, Eric, though he'd never been a true friend. Tormentor and owner, but never a friend. She thought of his parting words to her that last night and felt suddenly sick to her stomach.

"I'm sorry. I should have realized." Stewart put his hands in his coat pockets. A sheepish look suddenly crossed his face. He withdrew his hand, an orange now inside it. From his second pocket he produced another. "I forgot about these. The maid at the hotel gave them to me when I told her we didn't have time to take breakfast there."

Looking at his meager offering, he frowned. "But of course you're hungrier than this. I'd planned to buy you a meal once we arrived at Penn Station, but time got away from us. Perhaps I should check and see if there's a dining car on the train. . . ."

Charlotte snatched the fruit from his hand. "No, that's

quite all right. I'm really not that hungry. This is plenty."

She could feel him curiously watch her as she peeled the orange skin away. She tried not to choke as the tart juice trickled down her throat; food had little appeal right now. But she certainly didn't want him to spend his money on her. That only increased her guilt.

Thick silence, marred only by the rapid clickety-clack of the train's wheels, settled between them.

She must forget her past. Only then could she concentrate on the future.

two

Once they arrived in Ithaca, Stewart took her to a nearby restaurant. Charlotte was surprised that she was able to enjoy her baked ham and cranberries, or at least get them down without choking. The orange she'd eaten earlier had served to whet her appetite.

Afterward, Stewart grasped Charlotte's elbow and escorted her across the street to a small store. She stopped before he could assist her up the three painted white steps to the door.

"Oh, but what do we need here?"

"A decent change of clothes for you."

"Oh, no," she said, pulling back, "I can't let you do that."

He shook his head, his mouth thinning. "Myra, I know you don't have money. Don't be concerned. Michael will reimburse me if that's what's bothering you." When she still hesitated, he added, "You wouldn't really want him to see you in that condition, would you?"

Flustered, Charlotte looked down at the gap between the edges of her coat, which clearly revealed her high-necked evening gown, now torn and stained. She was glad she'd changed into this one the night of the sinking instead of the immodest ones Eric had insisted she wear. However, Stewart had a point; the state of the gown wasn't fit for meeting a "relation." Yet she felt uneasy about accepting monetary help from this man—a stranger. Wasn't that how things had started with Eric? But she could hardly approach Myra's uncle in such a manner.

"I suppose you're right," she reluctantly agreed.

"I left my Tin Lizzy with a friend," he said, opening the door and almost pushing her inside the store. "I think you'll do well without my aid. I'll be back for you shortly."

Tin Lizzy? Through the large display window at the front, Charlotte watched Stewart hurry down the board sidewalk and felt momentary panic. Surely he wouldn't leave her here?

Telling herself she was being ridiculous, she tore her gaze away from him and moved down the aisle. She sorted through the few ready-made dresses on the rack, deciding on a gray dress with thin black pinstripes and a few other things she needed. She hurried about her business, choosing to ignore the shopkeeper's narrowed gaze from the front of the store.

The brief bit of security she'd felt earlier in Stewart's company had evaporated as suddenly as morning mist, and again guilt pointed its invisible finger her way, branding her a felon. Charlotte was certain the storekeeper knew the truth. The stolen jewelry and deed burned a hole through her coat pocket. Any minute now she expected to feel a constable's hand roughly clap her on the shoulder.

She hastened to the front of the store and set her choices on the wooden counter.

"Mrs. Perkins at the boardinghouse next door will probably let you use the bath for a nominal fee," the storekeeper said in clipped tones, his eyes roving over her disheveled appearance with obvious disapproval. "Or you could try your luck at the hotel."

"No, thank you. If you have a washroom where I can change, that will suit me quite nicely," she murmured, unable to meet his eyes with her own.

Her gaze skittered to the folded newspaper on the counter. She felt dizzy when she read the headlines, screaming the news of the *Titanic's* passengers coming off the *Carpathia*. A photograph of a stricken couple walking next to their small son, who was being carried away on a stretcher, took up a good deal of space. Charlotte studied the picture, her eyes widening in recognition.

The storekeeper followed her rapt gaze. His gray brows drew down in a frown, and he intently peered at her face hidden behind the veil. "You were one of 'em, weren't you?" he asked more softly. "You were on the *Titanic*."

"I . . . ," Charlotte murmured, clutching the edge of the counter for support. "I'd rather not talk about it if you don't mind."

The disapproving look in his eyes changed to one of sympathy. "You can use the room at the back of the store, just down that aisle. I'll have my attendant bring you some water to wash with."

She nodded, her throat tight. She didn't want to remember that night. Not ever. She wanted to forget that the past few days existed, though she knew that would be impossible.

Charlotte found the tiny room, and a girl brought her a ceramic pan of water and a clean washcloth. Grateful, Charlotte nodded her thanks, then closed the door and turned the key. She stripped off her clothes, letting them fall to the floor at her feet. Gently she eased the wet washcloth over her bruised skin. Her body ached, but the cool water made her skin tingle.

Charlotte pulled on the new corset, petticoat, and black stockings. She donned the gray dress, relieved that it was a perfect fit. Lastly, she slipped her coat back on.

Carefully she combed her tangled hair, until it lay like a smooth, fiery curtain around her shoulders. With quick precision, she gathered it up and pinned the thick tendrils on top of her head, until she looked presentable. Though her hair could stand a thorough washing, it would have to do for now.

Studying her face in the cracked mirror on the wall, she saw that the bruise was fading. Yet it was still noticeable. She wondered if it would be too terrible to add a lipstick and container of powder to the bill. She wanted to look her best when she faced "Uncle Michael."

Charlotte hurried into the main room of the store and picked out the desired items. The storekeeper nodded gravely, adding them to the list, and she hastened back to the small room.

With a shaky left hand, Charlotte applied the rosy color to

her mouth, her eyes widening when she noticed in the reflection of the mirror the faint white mark on her third finger—evidence a wedding ring had once been there. It was at the bottom of the ocean now, having been relegated to her jewel box during her charade as Eric's sister. While on the *Titanic,* she'd worn several flashy rings—one of them on her ring finger to cover the mark.

She must purchase a pair of gloves. She only hoped Stewart hadn't noticed the mark on her finger. Charlotte knew from talking with Myra that she'd never been married or even engaged. It amazed Charlotte when Stewart had told her Myra's age. Myra had seemed so much younger, so innocent. Of course, she had been.

It was Charlotte who was defiled.

Clamping her teeth together, angry for remembering her past, which she'd so recently sworn to forget, Charlotte replaced her hat, then wrapped her soiled undergarments in the russet dress and tied the material in a knot. She left her dressing room, walked to the counter, and handed the bundle of clothing to the shopkeeper.

He looked at her, his thick brows lifted in surprise. "What do you want me to do with this?"

"Burn it," she said without hesitation and turned to the next aisle.

She plucked out a pair of white cotton gloves from a box on the shelf. Tugging them onto her hands, she tried to ignore the man's shocked reaction as he stared at the russet material he held, and then at her, then back to the dress. At last he went into a room behind him. When he returned, the velvet gown was nowhere in sight.

Stewart came inside and walked over to the counter.

"That'll be six dollars even," the storekeeper said.

"Six?" Stewart sounded surprised, and Charlotte looked at his broad back, instantly worried. Had she spent too much? Perhaps she shouldn't have added the lipstick and powder, though they had been inexpensive.

Stewart turned and caught sight of her. His gaze widened as it moved down her form, then back up to her face, no longer hidden by the veil. He slowly walked across the wooden plank floor to where she stood.

"Have you purchased everything you need?" His voice was gruff.

She nodded, uncertain. "I hope it wasn't too much."

"On the contrary. It was a lot less than I expected. Where are the rest of your things?"

"There isn't anything else."

He briefly closed his eyes and blew out an exasperated breath.

"Listen, Myra, you'll need to buy bedclothes, or whatever it is you women wear at night, and things of that nature. Another dress would be a wise investment as well. I doubt your uncle will have anything to loan you. And there isn't a store near his home, so you'll have to do your complete shopping at a later date. It would be wise for you to come well prepared."

"Of course." She looked away, embarrassed. She plucked the first cotton gown and wrapper off the shelf.

"Also another change of clothes," he added firmly when she was about to quit.

Charlotte swallowed. "I can make do with what I have." He started to argue, and she looked at him, her eyes begging him not to make an issue of it.

She wanted nothing more than to leave this place and this situation, which was growing more embarrassing by the moment—especially since it was being played out before a stranger, who watched with extreme interest. Charlotte had no doubt that soon the entire town would know of her visit here today.

Stewart's mouth narrowed, but he nodded and paid for her purchases. Picking up the bundle the storekeeper had wrapped with brown paper and twine, he hefted it under one arm and nodded toward the door.

A motorcar, its black sides and front gleaming, sat a short

distance from the store. A black top covered the two matching seats, a spare tire hung from the back, and a long window along the front sparkled in the sun.

Stewart grinned. "My Model T, or more affectionately known as my Tin Lizzy." He helped her up into the passenger side, threw the package on the backseat, and shut her door. She watched as he hurried to the front and bent to wind the crank. Soon the automobile choked to life, and he rushed to his place behind the wheel of the car.

"We're off!" he exclaimed, reaching behind him to the backseat to snatch up a battered plaid cap. He removed his bowler and replaced it with the cap, tugging the brim low over his forehead. He cast a wide grin her way before taking the wheel.

Pulling her veil over her face, Charlotte hid a smile at his childlike exuberance. The car rattled out of town onto a dirt road and through rolling green countryside that was similar to England, yet not quite the same. The houses, barns and fences were all made of wood rather than stone. And the bumpy dirt roads were wider here in America.

Charlotte was pleased with the differences. After all, she had engaged in an entirely new life, a new identity. How fitting that the surroundings would be distinctively different, as though she'd entered another world.

But you're not new, the familiar voice inside her head whispered, *and you can never be different.*

Furrowing her brow, she tried to ignore the cruel words.

Memory of the newspaper photograph she'd seen in the store came to mind. Had that really been Annabelle and Lord Caldwell?

Charlotte knew the two had romantic interests for one another, as everyone else had soon to discover. But they weren't married and certainly didn't have a child, as the paper implied. Yet if it was them and Lord Caldwell was alive, could that mean Eric had also survived the sinking? Had she missed him last night when she gathered with the others in the F section?

Closing her eyes, Charlotte bit the inside of her lip, not wanting to think about such things yet unable to stop. Would he look for her? Of course, he didn't know she'd taken on another identity, so that was a point in her favor. But what if he found out somehow? Eric was shrewd. Would he search for her and threaten her? Demand the deed and jewelry back if he had discovered them missing?

The questions were too much for Charlotte, and she wished for a diversion to end her traitorous thoughts. Hadn't she planned to forget all that was behind and strive for what was ahead? Whatever that might be. . .

Stewart turned at a sharp bend shaded by thick trees. A red heifer placidly stood on their side of the dirt road. Uttering a mild oath, Stewart whipped the wheel to the left. Bumping crazily on the seat, Charlotte gripped the door as the motorcar jounced into a ditch and came to an abrupt halt.

Stewart turned her way, his brow creased with worry lines. "Are you all right?"

"I think so." Though shaken, she felt otherwise unharmed.

Suddenly she began to giggle. The giggles turned into abrupt chuckles, finally ending in helpless laughter. Certainly she had nothing to laugh about, but she couldn't seem to stop.

Stewart looked at her as if she'd gone mad. His wide-eyed expression caused Charlotte to laugh all the more, until tears rolled down her cheeks.

"You see," she explained, when she could finally talk and be understood, "before we dodged the cow, I was hoping for a diversion. It seems I got one." She laughed again.

A slow grin spread over his mouth, causing the corners of his hazel eyes to crinkle. Soon he, too, was laughing, and for a few wonderful moments they forgot everything but the hilarity of the moment.

Stewart sobered, his admiring eyes never leaving her face. "You know, Myra, you're quite a woman."

Torn by his words, Charlotte looked away, no longer feeling like laughing. Hot tears pricked her eyes, and the bridge of her nose hurt. She blinked rapidly and stared up at the cow, which flicked its tail and studied her with soft brown eyes.

"Myra?"

The concern in Stewart's voice was her undoing, and she broke down, burying her face in her hands. She heard the swish of material sliding over leather as he moved closer. Strong arms enfolded her against his warmth, and she laid her head helplessly against his shoulder and cried, unable to stop. His hands went to her back and he stroked her shoulder blades, whispering words she couldn't hear or understand. But it didn't matter; they comforted her all the same.

Charlotte had no idea how much time passed, but finally the tears began to ebb, leaving her drained. Burrowing her face into his shoulder, she sighed. Here, nothing could touch her. An odd thought, since he was little more than a stranger.

Charlotte inched away from him and braved a glance upward. His eyes were soft, kind, and very concerned, making her feel like someone special. He pulled a white kerchief from his pocket and gently moved it over her eyes, being extra careful around the bruised skin, she noticed.

"All right now?" he asked.

She nodded. "I'm sorry—"

"Don't be. After what you've been through, your reaction is only normal. The tensions and trials you've undergone these past few days have been begging for release. To be honest, I've been waiting for something like this to happen. Only a person with a heart as hard as stone would be unaffected by the tragedy you endured."

"Why are you being so nice to me?" Charlotte asked from between stiff lips. "You don't even know me."

He appeared shocked by her stilted words, and instantly she wished she could take them back.

"I will never understand what you went through, Myra, since I didn't personally experience your pain that night. But I can sympathize and be there for you, and I can help you through this, if you'll allow me to do so."

She offered him a weak smile. Inwardly, she knew Stewart Lyons was a man who could be trusted. . . . Of course, she had thought Eric was, too, at first.

Shivering, she turned away and looked out the front window. "Thank you for the shoulder to cry on."

Sensing her sudden withdrawal, Stewart excused himself and stepped out of the motorcar. Now was not the time to delve. She was raw right now and needed time to heal.

A quick inspection showed him that his Tin Lizzy seemed to have fared well from its little mishap. He judged the distance to the road, then decided he would try to push the motorcar out of the ditch.

"Do you need me to get out?" Her soft voice came to him.

He shook his head. "No, I think I can manage." He didn't want to make her even more uncomfortable. He knew bruises must cover her body just as they did her face, judging from the way he'd seen her wince when the motorcar's wheel would hit a hole in the road. And her features had been strained throughout the train ride. Just what had happened to her onboard the *Titanic*?

God, please help me here. I don't want to scare her away. She seems frightened enough as it is. Help her to see that she can trust me. He looked down at his car. *And herculean strength to get my motorcar on the road again wouldn't be such a bad thing either, Lord,* he added wryly.

His mouth narrowing, he took off his jacket, tossed it on the hood, and rolled up his sleeves. Just as he put his hands to the grill and began to push, a young boy appeared over the grassy hill; he'd been searching for the cow, judging from the relief on his face when he looked in their direction.

"I could use some help," Stewart called to the stocky lad. The boy looked to be no more than thirteen, but strong for his age.

He ambled toward Stewart. His blue gaze remained glued to the car, and he ran one freckled hand over the shiny fender of the automobile. "Nice." He looked at Stewart. "This Minnie's fault, Mister?"

"Minnie?"

The boy's eyes cut to the cow and back.

Stewart nodded. "It seems Minnie was declaring territorial rights," he said with a touch of dry humor.

The boy's face reddened, and he looked to where the woman sat. "I'll help you, and we'll get you and your missus off in no time. I found the break in the fence, so Minnie's days of tourin' the countryside are over."

❧

Charlotte listened to the conversation through the opening above the door. When the boy referred to her as Stewart's wife, she waited for Stewart to explain. But he never did.

Why? Why didn't he clear up the misunderstanding? Could Charlotte really trust him? Yet what other choice did she have—she was a stranger in a strange land, an impostor.

Despite Stewart's assurances that she didn't need to, Charlotte stepped out of the motorcar, which suddenly felt stifling. She watched Stewart and the boy strain and grunt as they pushed the Model T up the three-foot embankment.

Soon they were on their way again, coughing and chugging down the dirt road, the boy walking up the hill behind them, leading the stubborn cow by a rope.

And throughout it all, the never-ending chorus echoed in Charlotte's brain. *Why?*

three

Stewart didn't say much for the rest of the drive, and Charlotte spent her time eyeing the neat orchards, the occasional farmhouse, and a beautiful lake shrouded by trees. Narrow gorges ran through outcroppings of tall rocks, and everywhere yellow forsythias and a few varieties of flowers that Charlotte didn't recognize splashed their bold colors against the vibrant green background.

Charlotte smiled, having always had a fondness for flowers. It may have been due to her childhood years, when she sold posies for two pence to the gentlemen who were escorting their lovely ladies down the narrow streets or through the park. There had been something special about the pretty flowers, which cheered the innocent little girl Charlotte had been, bringing color to her drab existence.

It had always been one of her fondest desires to someday own a small cottage with a huge garden wrapping around the back, sides, and front—a garden containing nothing but beautiful flowers. Her garden would be the most glorious in all the land, and many people would walk by her cottage just for the pleasure of seeing the many climbing rosebushes, hollyhocks, irises, lupines. . . .

"We're almost there." Stewart's words broke into Charlotte's reverie like a rock hurtling through the window of a glass house.

"Are you hungry?" he asked. "It's cook's day off, and you may have to fend for yourself. My place is close, though, and I know my housekeeper would love to serve you."

"I'd rather wait, thank you."

He nodded, and she resumed staring out the window, forcing her mind not to dwell on impossible fantasies.

"This is it," Stewart said a few minutes later.

Charlotte scanned the rich pastureland before her. Horses grazed beyond the white gate that paralleled the road. Stewart steered the motorcar around a bend onto a narrow lane; it was completely cloaked by thick trees that were just beginning to bud with dots and sprigs of yellow green. No sign of civilization could be seen—no house, no farm. The dirt road seemed to go on forever.

Charlotte felt uneasy. Up until their arrival in Ithaca, they had constantly been around people. But now they were totally alone. What guarantee did she have that Stewart wasn't a madman who accosted women in distress? That he wasn't as bad as Eric? Charlotte had learned too late that you can't determine a criminal by outward appearance. She knew little about this man—only what he'd told her.

And that meant nothing.

She'd lied through her teeth about her own identity. Suppose Stewart had done the same? Would some farmer wandering down the road find her body weeks from now in a nearby gully? But then again, he had known her name, or rather her assumed name, so she supposed he told the truth about being a friend of Myra's uncle. . . . But what if his words had merely been a pretense to waylay suspicion?

Charlotte gripped the edge of the seat, her nails sinking into the black leather. Strange that she now feared death, considering that she had tried to take her life only days ago. She had the craziest urge to throw open her door, jump out, and make a dash for it. Almost as if he knew the thoughts racing through her mind, Stewart glanced her way.

"If you'll look through the branches of those cottonwoods to your right, you'll see your first view of Larkin's Glen."

His calm voice coming so suddenly made Charlotte jump, but she turned her head to look through the thinning trees.

A sprawling multistoried house with white trim and gables stood sentinel over green pastureland, a thick forest of trees blanketing the background. Charlotte stared in wide-eyed wonderment, feeling as if she'd entered some sort of child's fairy tale. "Uncle" Michael was obviously a very wealthy man.

Her heart beat fast as Stewart parked the motorcar in the curving drive at the front of the house. This was insane! How did she ever think she could get away with this masquerade?

Stewart came around to her side of the car. For one anxious moment Charlotte cringed against the seat, ready to blurt the truth. *But,* reason argued, *what would you do then? You have nowhere to go, no money, no worldly possessions, nothing. Except for stolen diamonds and a deed to a house that doesn't belong to you. And Stewart is a lawyer. What makes you think he won't haul you off to jail if you were to admit your crime?*

Clenching her teeth, she laid her gloved hand in Stewart's strong one, allowing him to assist her from the car. She nervously scanned the front of the wood-and-stone house with its myriad of windows sparkling in the sun. As she watched, the front door opened, and a tall, gray-haired woman in a maid's uniform, replete with black dress and white apron, hurried down the four stone steps to greet them, words flying from her mouth.

"It's about time you got here, Stewart Lyons! Mr. Larkin's been pinin' away with worry ever since you left, though when he got your telegram, he was out of bed faster than a hound chasing a hare. 'Course, if you would have taken the buggy instead of that horseless carriage you're so fond of, you would have gotten back sooner. Never could understand what you saw in them noisy, smelly motorcars. I agree with Doc Sanderson. Give me a horse an' buggy any day. . . ."

"Ah, Mrs. Manning," Stewart said cordially when the woman paused for breath. "This is Myra Flannigan. Would you be so kind as to take her to her room and let her freshen up before she meets her uncle?"

Mrs. Manning grumbled something Charlotte couldn't quite make out, then looked her up and down with narrowed dark eyes. For one tense moment Charlotte was certain the unsmiling woman would point a finger in her face and yell, "Impostor!"

But she only gave a curt nod and muttered, "This way, Miss. It's no wonder you're tuckered out, what with Mr. Lyons dragging you all the way here in that horseless carriage of his, and with all you had to go through concerning the sinking. 'Course that boy never had a lick o' sense. . . ."

Once inside, Charlotte's hand clutched the carved mahogany banister like a lifeline, while she followed the talkative woman up a split-level set of dark-carpeted stairs. On the landing they turned to the right, and Mrs. Manning stopped complaining about Stewart and motorcars long enough to open one of five doors at the end of the wing.

"This is your room. Mr. Larkin had it done up special when he knew you was coming." Her tone implied that Charlotte had better like it if she knew what was good for her.

"I'm sure I'll love it," she murmured hastily.

The old woman narrowed her eyes again. "Dinner is at seven, and cook doesn't like it when people show up late."

So the cook had returned. Charlotte's arrival must have cut short the woman's day off. If the cook was anything like the woman she now faced, Charlotte would be certain to be seated at the table five minutes before the scheduled time.

"Thank you, Mrs. Manning. I'll just freshen up a bit." Yet what she really wanted to do was lie down. Her emotions had been in upheaval since the night of the sinking, like a boat tossed to and fro by tumultuous waves. However, rest was impossible at the moment. Michael was expecting her.

"There's a pitcher and basin inside, and a water closet at the end of the hall," Mrs. Manning said as she opened the door. A delicately carved white oak bedroom suite greeted Charlotte, the colors of the room a mixture of refreshing peach, the palest yellows, and soothing yellow-greens.

"It's lovely," Charlotte said, forcing the smile to remain on her lips.

Mrs. Manning grumbled something in reply, then pinned

Charlotte with another narrow gaze. "When you're ready to meet your uncle, he's in the family parlor downstairs—to the right of the staircase."

After the housekeeper left, Charlotte shut her eyes and wilted against the closed door. She stuffed her hands in the pockets of her coat, her gloved fingers making contact with the jewelry.

Frowning, she wondered if she should seek a hiding place for the stolen items and the deed. Or perhaps it would be best to leave them in her pocket for now. She doubted the stern Mrs. Manning would rummage through her clothing. But then again, the woman had looked at her with suspicion. . . .

Charlotte scooped the contents out of her pocket, the cool jewels seeming to burn through the thin material of her gloves and brand her for what she was—an accomplice to a thief.

Hurriedly she wrapped the diamonds and deed in a kerchief she found in the top bureau drawer. She searched the room with anxious eyes, her gaze lingering on the canopied bed. Swiftly she crossed the room, lifted the ivory chenille spread, and stuffed the bulky handkerchief deep under the mattress, wishing she could rid herself of its contents for good.

Turning, she caught sight of her reflection in the vanity mirror across the room. Her eyes widened at the image. The small mirror she'd used in the dimly lit storeroom hadn't revealed much. But this one told all.

The bruise showed again, a sickly yellow next to her shadowed eyes. Her hair, that she'd tried to pin so neatly, looked dirty and limp, and a few strands had escaped the pins to stick to her damp neck. She looked like she'd gone through a washerwoman's wringer, and though she felt as if she had, she certainly didn't want to meet "Uncle" Michael looking like this! No wonder the housekeeper had stared at her so strangely.

Charlotte spotted a silver-plated comb and brush set in a

gilded mirrored tray on the vanity. Grabbing the brush, she noted the initials M. F. on the back and realized they had been purchased for Myra's use. She plucked the pins from her hair and whisked the brush through her bright red locks, feeling guilty to be using things intended for another woman.

But, she reminded herself again, *Myra is dead. At least I can offer Michael Larkin a living niece. And I will never impose upon his generosity. Never.*

Determined, Charlotte removed her coat, hastily pinned up her hair, and liberally dusted her face with rice powder from a jar on the vanity. After spreading lip rouge on her pale lips, she stared at her solemn reflection.

It was time to meet the unknown uncle.

❧

On the downstairs landing, Charlotte stopped, her gaze traveling down the hall next to the stairs. She spotted a partially open door and, hearing the hum of voices, made her way in that direction. Light came from the crack between frame and door, and she paused a moment, then grasped the knob and pushed against the wood a smidgen to peek inside.

On the far side of what appeared to be a homey parlor, Stewart stood talking to someone sitting hidden from Charlotte's view in a large wingback chair. Dark, carved furniture sat neatly placed on the wooden floor. Deep reds and burnished golds gave the room a warm feeling, and on the paneled walls several paintings burst with glorious color, matching the hues in the large Persian rug.

Neither of the occupants noticed her presence yet, so Charlotte took closer inventory of the room, gathering the courage to walk inside. A beam of sunlight coming from a chink in the damask curtain that covered the floor-to-ceiling window directed her vision to the opposite wall, where a large-framed painting hung. The sunbeam played on the creation of a garden as seen through the opening of a white gate. Outside the picket fence the scene reminded her of winter, the colors drab, the trees bare, no sign of life in evidence.

But inside the open gate, colorful flowers bloomed in abundance, the grass was green, and butterflies flitted about the flower beds.

It was the most unusual piece of artwork Charlotte had ever seen. Something about the painting drew her from her place beyond the door to stand in front of it, without realizing she'd done so.

The canvas evoked beauty and serenity, while at the same time offering mystery. Even the name of the oil, *In the Secret Place,* which Charlotte could clearly see written at the bottom in small black script, increased her curiosity.

"My wife painted that not long after we married," a deep voice spoke from behind.

Charlotte jumped, then turned. A huge bear of a man—brawny, not fat—stood beside Stewart. He had thick red hair and a short beard, with strands of gray visible, and matching bushy eyebrows. Charlotte noted the piercing blue eyes that studied her, not unkindly, as closely as she studied him.

Uncle Michael.

"I–I'm sorry. I should have knocked, but the door was open, and when I saw this painting. . ." Again Charlotte turned toward it, more to hide the color that she knew had sprung to her cheeks than for any other reason. How embarrassing to be caught eavesdropping—for surely that's what Stewart and Michael must think!

He moved across the room to stand beside her, and Charlotte violently started. He was so big! At least twice as big as Eric. Did he have a mean streak as well?

"There, Lass. I'm not angered," he said with a lilting Irish brogue. "Consider this home your own, for it is just that." She looked at him and was relieved to see his face, though haggard, had creased into smiles. " 'Tis a pleasure to meet you at long last, Myra. You're the spitting image of me mother—your grandmother—may she forever rest in peace."

"And I'm happy to meet you, too. I'm glad to see you're feeling better." Charlotte allowed a brief smile of her own, thankful she so strongly resembled Myra. And what an unexpected stroke of luck that Charlotte reminded Michael of his mother! Perhaps keeping up this pretense wouldn't be as difficult as she'd thought.

"I'm looking forward to hearing you play after dinner. After reading Katie's letters praising your abilities on the pianoforte, I'm anxious to hear your music. Since Anna died two and a half years ago, the house has known nothing but silence."

Charlotte inwardly panicked, though she kept her face a smooth mask and tried to think of a way out of this sudden trap.

The only pastime she'd enjoyed in her miserable existence was the art of learning how to read and write. It was the one kind gesture Eric ever exhibited toward her, though his motives for teaching her had been purely selfish.

In their con games, Eric had forced her to play the part of a refined lady. "And," as he'd told her, "it simply would not do for a lady of ze social graces to be ignorant."

What had followed was months of strenuous work as he reshaped her from a "tavern brat" to a "semblance of a lady." From sunup till sundown, he had molded her, coached her, and many times cursed her when she didn't respond as fast as he wanted or forgot something he'd taught. Often she'd felt the back of his hand. But he'd never taught her to play a musical instrument; nor had she learned any of the other skills refined ladies were supposed to possess.

"I'm sorry," she finally murmured into the expectant silence, forcing a smile. "Truly I am. But," she held up the wrist that Eric had broken two years ago. "I hurt my hand some time ago, and it may be awhile before I can play. The night of. . . I injured it again several nights ago." At least this was no lie.

Michael's eyes clouded, and he slowly shook his head in remorse. "Ah, Lass. How thoughtless of me. Of course you've no mind to play after such a tragedy—hurt wrist or no! You must rest and regain your strength," he said, eyeing her intently, as though seeing her for the first time. His gaze lingered on her cheekbone, his bushy brows drawing downward.

Charlotte worried that he could see the bruise underneath the thick coating of powder and hurriedly turned to face the painting again. "Thank you."

"When you feel up to playing," he said, "you're welcome to do so at any time. Now come. You must be hungry. I'm certain Tildy wouldn't mind fixing a plate of cheese and fruit since you didn't arrive in time for lunch. Stewart—you come, too. And you'll stay to dinner as well? I can never thank you enough for bringing me niece to me."

"I can stay only a few minutes. I have to get back to the office," Stewart said, his tone strange.

Charlotte's gaze darted his way, unbidden. His narrowed eyes studied her with something akin to suspicion. The small smile faded from her lips.

"On second thought, I believe I will accept your invitation," he said slowly, his probing eyes never leaving hers. "I'll return later."

Charlotte looked away, trying to focus on what Michael was saying—something about the house and land—but she was uncomfortably aware of Stewart's piercing gaze on her back the whole time they walked from the parlor to the kitchen.

He knows I'm lying, she thought, her brow creasing with worry. *But how?*

❧

During the light brunch, Charlotte felt she must have misjudged Stewart. He was nothing less than gracious—smiling, drawing her out, even getting her to laugh once. There had been a few times when both men had asked personal questions to which she didn't know the answers. But she'd managed to field every one of them and easily turn the subject back to Stewart or Michael, depending on who asked the question.

After the meal, Michael excused himself, saying he needed to lie down, and encouraged Stewart to show Charlotte the garden. When Stewart opened the door at the back of the house, she gasped.

The garden was the same one she'd seen in the painting, yet the colors were more vivid than the oils in the canvas conveyed. It was still a little too early in the season for many plants to flower, but she could picture the apple trees blossoming near the picket fence and the sweet honeysuckle along the flagstone path in bloom. Daisies, lilacs, sweet peas, lupines, and roses would soon fill the sunny area. Purple pansies and a few other hardy flowers Charlotte couldn't identify ran riot in the flower beds now, adding cheer to the garden. Underneath a tree, two white, wrought-iron benches sat catty-cornered to one another. From the painting, Charlotte knew the cherry tree would soon be filled with pink blossoms, providing refreshing shade and color.

Charlotte closed her eyes, imagining the scene that would burst forth in a matter of weeks. Was she dreaming? Had her fantasy become reality? *In the Secret Place,* she thought, remembering the inscription at the bottom of the painting. *Could this be where I will find peace?*

Stewart lightly touched her elbow, and she jumped, her eyes flying open. He looked at her tenderly, and Charlotte's heart skipped a beat.

"The garden pleases you?" he asked.

"Oh, yes. It has always been my fondest desire to care for a garden such as this."

Stewart grew thoughtful. "Michael hires a gardener to take care of the lawns, but perhaps he might allot you a small section to tend. Would you like that, Myra? I could ask him."

Her spirits buoyant, Charlotte nodded enthusiastically. "Oh, yes!"

A thick tendril slipped loose from her upswept hair, brushing against her cheek and dangling to her shoulder. Stewart lifted his hand and touched the end of the silky strand. She flinched, taking a quick step backward. The tendril fell from his fingertips, and he lowered his arm.

"I must leave now," he said, his eyes unreadable. "There is paperwork I need to look over. Take care, Myra."

He turned to go. Before she could think about what she was doing, Charlotte put a tentative hand to his sleeve, stopping him. "Will you. . .will you still come to dinner?"

He looked at her in surprise, and she hastily dropped her hand from his arm. He'd been the first man who had ever shown her true kindness, and she didn't want him to walk out of her life. In that moment, Charlotte realized she desperately wanted his friendship. She'd never had a real friend, but instinctively knew his companionship would be highly prized.

His lips turned up at the corners, and one dark brow arched. "Would you like to have me come to dinner?"

She hesitated then gave a slight nod.

A twinkle lit his eye. "Then wild horses couldn't keep me away. But I really do need to take care of some business. I have other clients besides your uncle, and this case is due to go before the judge in less than a week." He took her hand in a brief clasp, gently brushing her fingers with a back and forth motion of his thumb before letting go. "I'll come back tonight. I promise."

Charlotte watched him stride to the gate. His broad-shouldered, athletic build reminded her of a farmer more than a lawyer. The fact that he'd taken time away from important business to meet her at the dock still filled her with awe.

Shaking her head, Charlotte moved toward one of the filigree benches, intending to soak up the warm sunshine. She grabbed the stray tendril of hair and twirled it around the pin on top of her head, her mind far away from her actions.

And yet. . .friendship with Stewart is unattainable. I could never tell him my secrets, she thought dismally. They were too dark, belonging in the far recesses of her mind, never to be spoken, never brought into the illuminating light of day.

Although she didn't want to face it, the fact remained: Stewart was on one side of the law, and she was on the other.

The beauty of the garden ceased to soothe her soul as shards of ice made quick stabs at her heart. Charlotte shivered, feeling as if she sat on the other side of the picket fence in the painting.

Winter's side.

❧

"Close the door, Stewart. I don't want our conversation overheard," Michael said gruffly after they'd left the dining room.

Stewart followed Michael into his study, closed the door, and took his usual place in the maroon, brass-studded chair next to the fireplace. Michael settled into the matching leather chair across from him and reached for his pipe on the small table at his elbow.

"Now, tell me everything," Michael said once he'd lit his pipe and taken several puffs.

Stewart studied the jumping yellow flames in the grate before turning his gaze to his friend. "Everything? What do you mean?"

"Ach, man!" Michael pulled the stem of the pipe from his mouth and slammed his other hand on the armrest, eliciting a lethargic glance from the old hound curled up on the hearth. "Do you think me blind or daft? I can tell when things aren't what they seem—especially under me own roof."

Stewart stalled, not wanting to air his own doubts and worry Michael. "So you don't think Myra has a headache? She did seem quiet at dinner—more so than usual." He had tried to catch her eye throughout the meal, but not once did she look his way. When Tildy served dried apple cobbler, Myra had risen with the excuse of a headache and hastened to her room.

Michael blew a whistling breath through his teeth. "For crying oot loud, I'm not talking about her headache. I want to know what happened to her. Her face looks as though she's been through a battle and came oot on the losing side."

Stewart nodded, furrowing his brow. The powder she wore did little to hide the bruise above her cheekbone—that was true. But he wasn't about to tell Michael that she looked much improved since the time he'd picked her up at Pier 54. "She was very vague about it when I inquired of her injuries. She only said it was a rough night."

"Now there's an understatement if ever I've heard one," Michael said brusquely, shaking his head. "What that poor lass had to endure. . .I cannot even fathom it. Yet she acts as though something more troubles her. Have you seen that look she sometimes gets? In all my days on this earth, I've never seen such terror in a person's eyes. At times she looks as though she thinks I may attack her."

Stewart nodded, remembering when he'd reached out to touch her tempting tendril of fiery hair earlier in the garden. His gesture had been without thought—as had her sudden withdrawal and the fear he'd seen crop up in her eyes, he was sure. Her reaction confused him, as had her lie about her hurt wrist. Not once had Stewart seen her favor that hand before they reached Larkin's Glen. . . .

There were many things about Myra Flannigan that didn't make sense. But soon, if he had his way about it, he would get to the heart of the matter. He would find out the truth.

four

"Top o' the mornin', Lass. I thought I'd find you here."

Michael stepped into the sunshine of the garden, a broad smile on his face.

Charlotte attempted a smile of her own. "Oh. Hello."

Since her arrival at Larkin's Glen a week and a half earlier, she had kept mostly to herself, a guilty conscience warring with her desire to make friends with Michael. Twice she'd eaten with him at the evening meal; but the latter half of this week he'd taken his meals in his rooms, too ill to come down. And before that, she'd made her excuses.

Grunting, he lowered himself onto the bench catty-cornered to hers. His face grew more florid, lines of strain pulling at his taut mouth.

Charlotte leaned forward in concern. "Are you all right?"

"Fit as a fiddle," he said, attempting a smile that didn't quite meet its mark.

"Maybe you should retire to your rooms," Charlotte offered helpfully. "Would you like me to get Tildy's husband?"

"Ach—I said I'm well! Couldn't be better." He shifted position slowly, propping his thick forearms on his trunklike legs, and leaned toward her. "Besides, I haven't spent much time with ye, Lass. I want to get to know me niece better."

His words sent shivers of apprehension trickling through Charlotte. She swallowed. "I'm not going anywhere. We can talk another time, if you'd prefer."

"But I don't prefer that at all." Hurt flickered in his eyes. "Unless, perhaps it's you who prefers that I go. . .?"

"Oh, no," she said quickly, though for him to leave was exactly what she did want. This man was kind, making her more uncomfortable in her charade. When she was in his

47

company, the guilt threatened to consume her. Yet at the same time, she didn't want to hurt him with her distance. Which was exactly what she had been doing, she realized with an inward sigh.

"Tell me about Katie," he said after an awkward span of silence. "Did she go home to the Lord easy? You didn't say much in your last letter."

Charlotte blinked, her mouth going dry. Katie? He must mean Myra's mother. "I—as easy as expected, I suppose," she murmured, plucking at her skirt.

A sad, faraway look entered his blue eyes. "Ah, me Katie. She was a spirited one, even as a young lass. Being the eldest, I had quite a job looking after her—as well as all four of me brothers and sisters—but she was me favorite." He sighed. "The youngest often are. I couldn't believe it when you wrote me of her sickness." His voice deepened with emotion. "And in one so young."

Charlotte remained silent, and he reached out and patted her clammy hand with his bearlike paw. "Never ye mind. You're here now, and here is where you will stay. It is my hope that we will become good friends."

Heart sinking, she managed what she hoped was an encouraging smile. "Good friends," he'd said. Yet little did this man realize the type of woman he harbored in his home.

Bad seed. Spawn. Illegitimate. All these names and worse Charlotte had heard as a child while growing up in the back rooms of a seedy tavern with a prostitute for a mother.

❧

"Hello!"

"Halloo, Stewart. What brings you here this fine day?" Michael asked with a grin.

Stewart watched as Myra turned on the bench in surprise. Her light green eyes grew wide, and a look close to pleasure covered her face, before it disappeared and her eyes went dull again.

Confused, he approached the two, forcing the smile to

remain on his face. "It's such lovely weather, I decided to play hooky and take Myra with me."

"Take me with you?" she asked, her voice whisper soft.

He nodded. "On a picnic."

"Oh, no, I couldn't. . . ."

Feeling like a smitten fool, Stewart held up the basket he'd wheedled his housekeeper into preparing. "Don't say no, Myra. I brought all the fixings—chicken sandwiches, cold potato salad, even apple pie. Your first all-American picnic."

Amusement flickered in her eyes, and her lips tilted up a fraction at the corners, making his heart threaten to pound out of his chest.

"You do make it hard to say no," she admitted.

"Then don't," he said, his smile widening. He held out a hand. "Please?"

Her brow furrowed in indecision, and Stewart watched as her eyes clouded again. What was she thinking? Why did she so often get that resigned yet pained look—as though she carried a satchel full of deep worries?

"Go on, Myra. It will be good for you," Michael urged.

"Well, perhaps," she relented.

Stewart felt like cheering, but instead offered her a hand up. She hesitated, then accepted his aid. Her hand was soft and warm and fit perfectly inside his. As if it had been designed that way. Stewart cleared his throat of the funny lump that had come into it.

"I have the perfect place in mind. A place I often visited as a child."

Myra sent him a faltering smile. "All right. Actually, I've never been on a picnic."

The uncomfortable needle-prick of doubt stabbed him. Never been on a picnic? Briefly he remembered his short stay in England six years ago, when Myra and her family had taken him riding over the English countryside, then stopped in the meadow for a light repast. At sixteen, he'd thought her taller as well and had been surprised at how short she stood when he'd met her at Pier 54 over a week ago. She looked like Myra. . .yet she seemed so different from the lively sprite he'd once known.

꙳

Stretching out, Charlotte rested her palms against the grassy, tree-lined bank next to the rushing water. A small waterfall, its droplets sparkling iridescent in the air, fell from the rocks bordering the stream on the other side. She eyed a loon that lazily glided by. The sunshine made its colorful feathers more vibrant, its head and neck glowing emerald. The bird floated by, ignoring them, as if it didn't have a care in the world.

"Myra, where are you?"

Stewart's low voice brought her out of her musings, and she turned, feeling almost guilty. "I'm sorry."

"Don't be." His dark brows drew down in a frown. "I'm glad you're finally relaxing. You've been strung as tight as a string on a fiddle since I've met you."

She lifted one eyebrow, feeling her lips tilt at the corners. "A fiddle?" This was the second time she'd heard that word today.

"Like a violin," he said. "A musical instrument."

"And do you play this fiddle?"

His small grin became an all-out smile, sending strange tremors through Charlotte's heart.

"You bet I do. And it just so happens I brought it with me. Would you like to hear me play?"

Amused at the little-boy appeal on his face and in his voice, Charlotte nodded. "Of course."

She watched as he rose from the blanket, dusted off the seat of his pants, and strode to the Tin Lizzy. He withdrew a black case from the backseat, returned to his spot several feet from her, and sank to the ground again.

Taking a stringed instrument from the case, he positioned it under his chin. The dark wood gleamed rich in the sunlight. He picked up a bow and ran it across the strings a couple of times, moving the fingers of his other hand along the neck. The still air was racked by discordant notes, sending the loon, wings flapping, skittering across the stream.

Stewart looked at her sheepishly. "My apologies. It's been awhile." He turned the pegs on the side of the neck, ran the bow across the strings, and nodded. "Okay, here we go. Any requests?"

"Something lively." Charlotte leaned back on her elbows and crossed her ankles. She listened with interest to the rollicking tune, the toes of her boots tapping against one another. Though Stewart couldn't be called an accomplished musician, he played with enthusiasm, clearly enjoying himself.

Afterward she smiled. "That certainly was lively."

" 'Oh Dem Golden Slippers' was the first song my grandfather taught me. He was the real musician in the family." One side of his mouth turned upward in a rueful grin. "I received the brains, not the talent."

"Oh, but I enjoyed it," Charlotte said, and meant it. Though he'd struck an off note now and again, his music had been freeing, helping her to relax. "Play another."

"Do you really mean that?" he asked incredulously.

"Yes."

His brow reflected puzzlement for a moment, then he smiled. "I don't know too many new ones. This is one of your uncle's favorites from years gone by."

The wailing notes carried on the still air. A V-formation of blackbirds cawed as they flew past, adding their own sound. Charlotte stiffened, feeling as if she'd suddenly been turned to stone. Her mouth went dry as dust, and her heart seemed to stop in her chest—then painfully soared with rapid beats.

Stewart continued to play, lost in his music, a half-smile on his face as his brow pulled down in concentration. In the middle of the song his gaze met Charlotte's. Instantly he pulled his bow away and lowered the instrument, his eyes filling with concern. "Myra, what's wrong?"

Charlotte shook her head slowly, for a moment unable to

articulate any words. "I've heard that before."

"You look as if you may swoon. Here, lay back before you fall down." He lowered her to the blanket, then hurried to the edge of the water. He returned and laid a wet kerchief on her brow. "The tune is an old American one, but I'm certain it could have made its way into England at some point."

"My–my mother used to hum it," Charlotte whispered. A picture of her mother stirring their meager meal in the kettle on the hearth while sadly looking into the bubbling contents and humming that tune flashed across her mind.

"Well, then, there you have it. She probably heard your uncle sing it when he visited England. 'Oh, My Darling Clementine' was a popular song in its day. Still is."

Charlotte's heart turned to a solid lump within her breast, making it difficult to breathe. "What did you say the name of that was?" she asked hoarsely.

He repeated it, and she closed her eyes, swallowing hard.

Clementine. Her mother's name.

❧

On the drive home, Myra sat in silence, and Stewart grew worried. This impromptu outing hadn't gone as planned. Why had the song upset her so? His lawyer's mind clicked into gear.

He had wanted to relieve the nagging suspicion that she wasn't Myra at all, but someone playing the role of Myra. Yet the picnic had just reinforced his doubts. If she were an impostor, the question remained—why? Why was she playing a role? Michael's money didn't seem to be an attraction. She flat refused Stewart when he'd told her to augment her wardrobe with another dress while in Ithaca. In fact, she seemed unwilling to spend a cent of Michael's money.

Stewart's hands clenched the wheel, his knuckles turning white. Might she be a swindler who'd learned her craft well? In his profession he'd run up against women acting the damsel in distress who'd turned out to be the opposite—the villain, not the victim.

Stewart glanced Myra's way, narrowing his gaze. She stared

out the window at the front, tendrils of bright red hair flying around her face from the cool breeze. Her gloved hands lay clasped in her lap, and her eyes were clouded with that look of pain that he'd seen so often touching her features.

Again the strong desire to protect surged through him, as it had since the rainy night they'd met. He determined to prove her innocence in his own mind. She's been through a great deal, he silently reasoned. That's why she's so vulnerable at the moment and the song upset her so. And there must be a logical explanation for all the other inconsistencies as well. Six years was a long time. It wasn't so unusual that she would have forgotten him, and perhaps he'd only imagined her being taller.

He forced a smile and pointed at a white spire breaking through the tops of some oak trees. "That's the church Michael and I frequent."

"It's lovely," she said in a monotone.

"Perhaps this Sunday you'd care to go with me? Michael wasn't able to attend last week because of his health, and I didn't think of asking you—"

"Oh, no," she broke in. "I—I've nothing to wear."

Stewart's brow pulled down in a frown. "The dress you have on is perfectly acceptable for a worship service, Myra. It's a small country church."

She bit her lip. "I suppose."

Charlotte looked toward the white clapboard building that came into clear view as Stewart rounded a corner. She certainly wouldn't have to worry about running into Eric there, she thought wryly. If he were alive, church would be the last place he'd visit. Her teeth sank deeper into her lip, a fear she couldn't name rising up and threatening to consume her as she stared at the quaint building with the rows of hollyhocks growing along the side.

Briefly she closed her eyes. Her emotions seemed to be getting the best of her, as they had since the *Titanic* went down. Why else had she acted in such a preposterous manner over that silly song? And the church was just a building, after all. She had no reason to feel so anxious.

She turned away from the simple structure and looked at Stewart. "Is there. . ." She swallowed to maintain composure. "I'd like to locate a list of *Titanic* passengers who survived."

He shot a glance her way. "I'm certain that could be arranged. My secretary keeps clippings of newsworthy events. A hobby he's acquired." He shook his head. "I'd forgotten you said you made friends while on the voyage. I've been remiss in not acquiring a list of survivors for you before now. My apologies."

She attempted a smile. "You've nothing to apologize for. Uncle Michael told me you've been busy with your case."

Stewart nodded, his mouth grim. "A most difficult one, but all turned out well in the end."

"Oh?"

"A sly young woman deceived her family into thinking my client had perpetrated the crime. It was my duty to prove her false—a difficult task, but one well worth the effort. Helping to mete out justice is one of the reasons I chose to become an attorney. Too many criminals go unpunished."

His mouth narrowed, and his hand slammed the wheel, startling Charlotte. "The guilty need to know there will be repercussions for wrong actions, or the innocent will forever be at risk," he stated, a tic jumping near his jaw.

"Oh." Charlotte's throat tightened, and she found it difficult to draw breath. "But is there no middle ground? Are the guilty just that—guilty?"

He darted another glance her way. "What do you mean?"

"Sometimes. . ." Charlotte inhaled deeply, rubbing the fingers of one hand with the forefinger and thumb of the other. "Sometimes there's more to a situation than meets the eye, surely. What if the guilty party in question was forced by another to commit a wrongful act?"

One side of his mouth turned upward in a grin. "You're beginning to sound like a lawyer."

"I knew a barrister once," she said, turning her gaze to the front, afraid he'd see the guilty look in her eyes. Edgar Flottingham had been one of Eric's victims, and she'd been the bait. "He shared some of his cases with me."

She could feel Stewart's eyes on her, but didn't look his way. "Principles are principles," he said, his voice grim. "People know right from wrong, unless they've spent a life in crime. Then their hearts harden, and it's difficult for them to discern evil. They grow accustomed to it and can no longer differentiate between the two—right and wrong."

Strange that never happened to me, Charlotte mused. *I always knew Mum's life and mine were evil—the townspeople never let us forget it, with their averted eyes and snide remarks.* Yet being embroiled in the evil Eric inhabited had been her worst nightmare.

"No one is 'forced,' " Stewart continued. "It's just as easy to say no as it is to say yes."

"Is it?" Charlotte's head snapped his way. "And what do you really know of such things? What if fear of death were a factor in such a decision?"

"Fear of death?"

"Of being murdered. I've heard there are such cases."

"You mean self-defense?"

"Not exactly." She rubbed her forefinger with more rapid strokes. "I mean when someone forces a person to commit an evil act, threatening that person's life if the person doesn't comply."

Stewart threw her a puzzled look. "Such cases are rare, I would think. But in any event, I would rather trust the Lord to protect me and remain upright than bow my knee to evil."

Her chin lifted a fraction, and she shifted on the seat. "That's easy for you to say. You have lived comfortably in a good home and were raised by two loving parents. But not everyone has had that advantage. Not everyone knows God as you apparently do, either."

Stewart veered the motorcar to the side of the dirt road,

coming to an abrupt halt. He exhaled deeply, then turned her way, his hands still on the wheel. "Why so upset, Myra? From what Michael told me, you had the same advantages I did. And certainly the fate of the accused isn't anything for you to be overly concerned about."

She shook her head, clutching her hands tighter in her lap, still refusing to look at him.

He tapped his thumbs on the steering wheel. "Everyone has a conscience. Even those who don't know the Lord, as you and I do. There's always been right, and there's always been wrong. And when people choose, of their own free will, to step outside the boundaries of the law, they are convicted. They may not admit to the conviction, but deep inside, they know they are wrong."

"And so your answer is to put them in a cell and throw away the key," she said bitterly.

He shook his head in frustration. "You have a good heart, Myra. But would you feel safe if those kinds of people were running loose? People who commit crimes against society— for whatever reason? It's my job to serve the community by helping to see that they are put away."

"I thought you wanted to help people," she murmured. "It sounds as if, in your mind, you've already convicted them without benefit of a trial."

"I do want to help. . .both the victims and those wrongly accused. The innocent should never be made to suffer for another man's crime. If I have any suspicions concerning a would-be client's innocence, I refuse the case. This isn't about money for me; it's about justice."

Charlotte dared a glance his way, wondering at the sudden bitter tone of his voice. He stared straight ahead, his mouth turned down at the corner, a dark scowl covering his face.

Shivering, she looked away, sliding closer to the door. She knew she was in the wrong, so why had she gotten so defensive? And how long till he discovered her lie? What would he do then? The answer to that question was obvious, considering their conversation. Charlotte could almost hear the clang of prison doors slamming shut.

There would be no mercy.

As the motorcar clattered and coughed up the drive leading to Michael's house, Charlotte noticed a black carriage parked out front, led by two beautiful bay horses.

"That's Doc Sanderson's buggy," Stewart stated, a thread of alarm evident in his voice.

Stewart brought the Model T to a shuddering stop beside the carriage. The horses snorted and pawed the ground, straining at the reins; the carriage shot forward a few inches, and for a moment it looked as though the bays would take off.

Quickly Stewart stepped out and went around to the other side of the car, all the while speaking soothing words to the frightened animals, his hands lifted in the air as in a show of surrender. Before he could help Charlotte out, she had exited and was halfway to the house.

As they entered the foyer, a portly man with gray hair and matching bushy sideburns alongside his face and jaws came down the stairs. He held a black bag in one hand. "Stewart, glad you came." He looked at Charlotte. "Who's this?"

"You've heard Michael talk of his niece, Myra Flannigan. Myra, this is Dr. Sanderson." Stewart's expression grew grim. "Is it Michael?"

The doctor gave a curt nod.

"Bad?"

"He's better now." Doc pinned Charlotte with his dark gaze. "Miss Flannigan, I wonder if I could have a private word with you?"

Charlotte bit the inside corner of her lip, then nodded. She would prefer that Stewart stay, despite the uneasiness between them, but obviously the doctor's request didn't include his company.

Stewart turned to her, all signs of former anger gone. "I have some briefs that need my attention. I'll try to come back later this evening, if you should need me. Okay?"

"Yes." Charlotte gave him a grateful smile.

"Stewart," the doctor drawled, "if you would kindly not frighten my horses when you leave here with that infernal machine you insist on driving, I would be ever so grateful."

Stewart's lips twitched, and his eyes glowed with mirth. "Doc, mark my words, one day motorcars will replace the horse and buggy for transportation, and you'll have no choice but to obtain an automobile of your own. Or be left out in the cold."

"Harrumph! That will be the day!" Doc shook his head, his whiskered jowls quivering with the motion. "It's a passing fancy—nothing more. The horseless carriage will fade away like all the other ridiculous inventions that weren't worth a half penny! People have more sense than to replace the dependable horse and buggy for one of those noisy, smelly contraptions."

"We shall see, Doc. We shall see." Stewart's grin widened as he tipped his hat at Charlotte. "Until this evening."

Doc stared after Stewart as he exited the door. "Boy hasn't a lick of sense sometimes. Always knew he would be a stubborn one, ever since I caught him stealing those chicken eggs," he said under his breath.

Charlotte fixed him with an unbelieving stare. "Stewart stole chicken eggs?"

"Hmmm?" Doc turned to Charlotte, as though just remembering her presence. "Stole chicken eggs. . .yes, he did. Of course, he was only five at the time. Thought by taking the eggs he could save the baby chicks' lives, fool boy." His thick lips turned upward into a fond smile. "He makes a fine attorney, though—has a caring heart and is highly intelligent. All in all, he's grown into an upstanding young man! Just dimwitted when it comes to that machine of his."

Charlotte hid a smile. She tried to imagine Stewart as a five-year-old child. His hair probably had been a shade or two lighter, and she could imagine a curly lock of it falling over his forehead. Big hazel eyes looking up innocently, the stolen brown eggs held in grubby hands. She envisioned a wide, gap-toothed smile splitting his face. She wondered if he might have had freckles as a boy, though there was no sign of them now. . . .

"Perhaps we should retire to the front parlor for our talk?" the doctor suggested, after checking his silver pocket watch and replacing it in his vest pocket.

"Oh, of course." Charlotte snapped out of her musings. "Right this way, Doctor."

However, he was already ahead of her and opening the parlor door. Mrs. Manning came inside as Charlotte sat down in a stiff chair, and Doc took the wingback.

"Will you be wanting your usual, Doc?"

He gave a curt nod. "Stout enough to peel the wallpaper, no cream or sugar."

Mrs. Manning turned to Charlotte. "And you'll be wanting tea, Miss? With lemon?"

"Yes, please." After the housekeeper had left the room, Charlotte looked at Dr. Sanderson. "I take it you've been here often. I can only hope your visits have been mostly social rather than professional."

"A little of both, I'm afraid." Doc swiped a weary hand over his bristly jaw. "Miss Flannigan, since you're your uncle's only kin, I feel the need to confide in you concerning my findings."

Charlotte fidgeted, the lie she lived again pricking her conscience. She had no right to hear about Michael's condition. Still, a feeble bond had formed between them, and Charlotte wanted to know just how bad things were.

"Is he. . .is he going to die?"

"He undoubtedly wishes so."

Charlotte moved back against the chair in shock, her shoulder blades making contact with the wood. "What do you mean?"

The doctor exhaled a long breath, a defeated expression covering his face. But before he could speak, Mrs. Manning returned with the refreshments.

Hands in her lap, Charlotte slid a thumb and forefinger over the gloved fingers of her other hand, watching. It seemed the housekeeper took more time than usual setting the cup and saucer just so, placing the plate of triangle sandwiches at a precise angle on the piecrust table next to Charlotte, pouring a thin trickle of tea into the cup. . . .

"Thank you, Mrs. Manning," Charlotte said, impatient with her snail-like movements. "I will take care of the rest. You may go now."

The housekeeper straightened, her mouth dropping open then slamming shut like the jaws of a snapping turtle. "Very well, Miss," she said, shooting one of her narrowed gazes Charlotte's way.

Positive that if she'd not done so before, she'd now made herself an enemy, Charlotte concentrated on the doctor and paid little attention as the housekeeper whisked out of the room and closed the door with more force than necessary.

"Pardon me for saying so, Miss Flannigan, but that wasn't a smart thing to do. Mrs. Manning has been here almost as long as Larkin's Glen has. She cares a great deal about your uncle."

Remorse filled Charlotte, though impatience took the upper hand. "Yes, you're right, Doctor. I'll talk to Mrs. Manning later. Now, back to what you were saying, why should Uncle Michael wish to die? Is his condition so serious that nothing can help him?"

Dr. Sanderson emitted a long sigh, and from the pained expression filling his eyes, Charlotte could see that Mrs. Manning wasn't the only one who cared deeply about Michael. The doctor took a sip of his coffee, then set the cup down, again fixing her with his solemn gaze.

"While it's true that he suffers frequent stomach problems and other maladies associated with the digestive system," the doctor explained, "what is eating your uncle's insides cannot be remedied with a simple tonic or even the best of medical care. What Michael suffers from is guilt."

"Guilt?" Sitting forward, Charlotte furrowed her brow at the strange statement. "Whatever would a kind man like my uncle have to feel guilty about?"

"Ah, Miss Flannigan, I cannot divulge a confidence, as much as I wish I could confide in you, for I see that you have a caring heart concerning your uncle. But I can tell you this: Your uncle has lived with an old regret for many years, but even more so since his wife passed away. A shame of his youth has tortured his soul, and that is why he wishes for death. He tried to rectify his mistake but was unable to do so, and now he wallows in the sins of his past. That is what tears him apart. And I believe the bitter remorse he harbors is affecting his health as well."

Charlotte stared, trying to absorb his words and make sense of them. Certainly she could understand remorse and the inability to rectify a mistake—that scenario was the story of her life. What she couldn't understand was that someone as benevolent, someone who obviously loved God as much as Michael did, could be afflicted with such a problem.

"The reason I'm telling you this, Miss Flannigan, is because I think your presence here is a godsend. Perhaps if Michael can concentrate on you, he will forget, or at least put into the background, that which torments him."

"I see." Charlotte lowered her gaze, studying the seams of her white-gloved fingers.

"Michael mentioned that you have kept to yourself most of the time since you've arrived at Larkin's Glen. I'm asking you as his friend, as well as his physician, to please consider spending more time with your uncle. I think by doing so, it could be beneficial to his health."

Slow heat flooded Charlotte's face. "I understand, Doctor," she said, lifting her gaze to his. "And I will try to make myself more accessible in the future. I do care about his welfare."

He smiled. "I knew I could count on your cooperation, Miss Flannigan." He downed the rest of his coffee, though it must have been piping hot, and checked his pocket watch again. "I must be going. I need to check on another patient while I'm in the vicinity."

"I'll see you to the door." Charlotte started to rise, but the doctor raised a hand, palm outward.

"No, don't bother. Sit and enjoy your tea. You haven't yet touched it. Good day, Miss Flannigan. I'll check on your uncle again tomorrow."

After the doctor bustled out of the room in his quick, no-nonsense way, Charlotte allowed her "acting mask" to slip and fell back against the chair, staring at the light brown liquid cooling in the fragile teacup. She would have to put aside her fears and spend time with Michael for his sake. . . . And if she were found out as a result of doing so?

Charlotte shuddered and momentarily closed her eyes. After a long moment, she straightened, inhaled deeply, and fixed her face into a pleasant expression. Then she rose from the chair, intending to go in search of the rebuffed housekeeper.

A crash splintered the air, and Charlotte hurried to the door.

five

A young, dark-haired maid in a black-and-white uniform knelt on the floor, picking up pieces of broken pottery that lay next to a small table. Hearing Charlotte's footsteps, she turned her way.

"Oh, I'm sorry, Miss! I bumped into the table while I was dusting. I'm afraid I broke a vase," she said needlessly, anxiety clouding her brown eyes.

Charlotte looked at the broken shards, then at the maid. "What's your name?"

"Beth. This is my first day here." She stood, wringing her hands. Her expression made it clear that she thought it would be her last day in Michael Larkin's employ as well. "I–I hope this wasn't too expensive," she murmured.

Tears filled the girl's eyes, and when she lifted a hand to brush at them, Charlotte saw a trickle of red.

"You've cut your hand," she said, furrowing her brow. "Go tend to it. I'll take care of this."

Beth looked undecided, and Charlotte offered an encouraging smile. "Go on."

"Thank you, Miss."

As Charlotte gathered the jagged pieces and put them on a nearby enamel tray, a shadow fell over her. She looked up to see a very disapproving Mrs. Manning.

"An accident," Charlotte said, feeling a quiver run down her back. The other woman's lips tightened while her gaze went from the broken pottery in Charlotte's hand to the tray on the table.

"That platter is over one hundred years old," Mrs. Manning said with a sniff. "And the vase was almost that."

Charlotte straightened. "I'll get a broom."

"That's what the hired help is for, Miss." By her tone, she let Charlotte know she didn't approve of her interference.

Charlotte took a deep breath, remembering her interrupted errand. "Mrs. Manning, I want to apologize for the abrupt way I spoke to you in the parlor. Fear for my uncle's welfare lent a bite to my tongue. I realize you also care about his condition."

For a brief moment, the woman's features softened, and Charlotte was amazed at the change. Why had she never noticed it before? Mrs. Manning was in love with Michael!

The housekeeper gave a stiff nod, looking away. "Thank you, Miss. I'll clean the rest of this now."

There was nothing more to say. Charlotte moved toward the stairs, deciding it was time to visit Michael and put her promise to the doctor in practice.

❧

Two days later, Charlotte stood at the open window, one hand at shoulder level, clutching the green damask curtain. The rattling and chugging of a motorcar broke the peace of the country morning. Several birds in a nearby oak tree flapped their wings, twittering as their quiet was disturbed. A squirrel on the ground chattered angrily, then raced up another oak and leapt onto the roof of the house.

Biting the inside of her lip, Charlotte watched as Stewart's black vehicle bounced around the bend and up the path, white smoke billowing from the back. Her clammy hands went to the skirt of her pinstriped dress, and she smoothed the silvery gray folds with nervous pats. A cuckoo clock downstairs sounded the ninth hour.

Taking a deep breath, Charlotte forced her steps away from the window and woodenly walked down the stairs to meet Stewart.

She reached the landing as Mrs. Manning opened the front door and let him inside. His eyes lit up on sight of Charlotte, and she felt momentary satisfaction that she passed his inspection—though she wore the same dress she'd been wearing every day since her arrival. But the fear that had gripped her all morning attacked her mind again.

Was she insane to accept Stewart's invitation? The other night, when he'd come after the doctor's visit, he'd been so comforting, so supportive, that Charlotte found herself agreeing to go to church with him before she could think twice. She supposed she could have come up with an excuse and canceled; however, if she refused to attend, she might be looked upon with suspicion, since Myra was a Christian. And yet. . .

"You look lovely," Stewart said when she hesitated. "We really should leave now. I had trouble starting my motorcar, which is why I'm late."

Charlotte allowed the mask to slip over her face, and she offered him a bland smile as he escorted her to his Tin Lizzy. "You don't own a horse and carriage for such emergencies?"

He shook his head ruefully. "I traded in the carriage, though I do have a horse. I didn't think it would be wise for us to ride together in the same saddle," he added with a teasing grin. "Some might misconstrue such a thing and think I'm abducting a beautiful lady to secrete her away in my manor."

Charlotte's heart jumped within her chest, and hastily she looked toward the vehicle. His forthright way of speaking no longer surprised her, though she wondered if she'd ever grow accustomed to his banter. "I don't really mind the. . .Tin Lizzy did you say it was?"

Stewart nodded, a proud gleam coming into his eyes as he straightened and thrust out his chest a tad. "It came out last year. One of the finest—a Model T touring car."

Charlotte stepped up and slid into the long black seat, and Stewart closed her door, then went to the front and turned the crank. When the engine caught, he ran to his place behind the wheel, and they were on their way.

The cool breeze wafting Charlotte's hot face did little to stem her anxiety, which grew the closer they came to the white building with hollyhocks at the sides. The steeple came into view, and she hoped they could slip in the back unnoticed, find a seat in the last row, then slip out before anyone was the wiser. . . .

The motorcar chugged up the path, frightening the horses tethered to a fence. They whinnied, shaking their heads and tossing their dark manes. A barking spotted dog bounded from behind the church building, came to a stop a few yards from where Stewart had pulled in, and continued to bark at them. A sudden backfire, as loud as a cannon's blast, startled the dog, which shot toward the back of the church, yipping. Two men poked their heads out the front door and stared, frowns on their faces.

So much for sneaking in without anyone noticing, Charlotte thought wryly. Stewart didn't seem to notice the havoc his motorcar had created. He smiled her way before sliding out his side and coming around the car to assist her.

"Are you the only one who owns one of these?" Charlotte asked quietly as they walked up the four steps to the door. "I don't see any others."

"I know a few people who own them and use them for recreational purposes, but they also have horses and carriages."

They found a seat in the fourth pew from the back just as the opening hymn ended. Tense, Charlotte clasped her gloved hands in her lap and stared straight ahead, jumping slightly when she felt Stewart's large hand cover hers and give her fingers a squeeze. She looked at him, and he offered a reassuring smile, then winked at her before removing his hand and focusing his attention on the soberly dressed gentleman at the front. The man opened a black book on the podium and began to read.

Throughout the service, Charlotte looked neither left nor right, feeling stares directed her way from all over the small building. Could the people see through her? Did they know what kind of woman sat in their midst? Oh, why had she agreed to come?

Suddenly the minister's words caught and held her attention.

". . .And so we know that the precious blood of Jesus washes us white as snow. Only His blood can cleanse us from our sins, but we have to be willing to be cleansed. Like the woman who was caught in the act of adultery. . ." His gaze roamed the congregation and fastened on Charlotte; shivers traveled down her spine. ". . .Until she met Jesus, she was doomed. But His saving grace delivered her from death, as surely as it will deliver you or me, and He forgave her, as surely as He forgives anyone who comes to Him with a repentant heart. . . ."

Charlotte sat unblinking, her eyes beginning to burn. Annabelle had talked to her once about Jesus' blood cleansing sins, but Charlotte didn't understand. How could God forgive such a woman as that adulteress? How could God forgive Charlotte herself?

Blood pounded in Charlotte's ears, drowning out the minister's words. She rubbed her fingers harder with thumb and forefinger, pulling the material of her glove off a few inches. Again Stewart's warm hand covered hers, though this time he didn't look at her. Nor did he remove his hand.

Charlotte relaxed, comforted by his touch.

After the minister finished speaking, he asked for those who had made a decision to accept Christ to come forward. Charlotte watched as an ox of a man in the plain garb of a farmer, his shoulders shaking with suppressed sobs, shuffled to the front and dropped to his knees on the wooden floor in front of the pulpit. The sight moved her, and something whispered to her heart to do the same—to give her life to Jesus.

Uncomfortable, she averted her gaze, relieved when the service ended. Several women headed her way, their eyes curious, and Stewart gave her hands another squeeze before rising to face them. Charlotte stood, moving close to his side.

"Mrs. Boswell, Mrs. Cosgrove, how good to see you this fine morning," Stewart said. "You remember Michael mentioning he had a niece coming to visit? This is Myra Flannigan."

The stout woman with dark hair and a hat loaded with purple flowers beamed at Charlotte, while her rail-thin, white-headed companion only nodded. "Oh, how wonderful to meet you at last," the dark-haired woman said. "And this is my mother, Mrs. Cosgrove."

"How do you do," Charlotte said through stiff lips, painfully aware of the older woman's unsmiling stare. Did she somehow know Charlotte was a fraud?

Others came to greet her, and she grew flustered by all the faces and names. Except for Mrs. Cosgrove, everyone seemed quite nice and willing to accept her. Of course, they didn't know she wasn't the sweet Myra they believed her to be.

Charlotte felt Stewart's gaze on her face. He must have sensed her strain, for his hand lightly went to her back in a show of support. "Ladies, we must go now. Michael is waiting."

After several sympathetic comments and pats on her arm, they allowed Stewart to take her outside.

Charlotte deeply breathed in the fresh air, grateful to escape. They were almost to the motorcar when a shout stopped them.

"Stewart! I say, wait up old man!"

Charlotte turned to see a middle-aged gentleman in a gray suit waving at them from the church steps as he ran down them.

Stewart exhaled loudly. "A client. He may have something important to tell me." His gaze turned to Charlotte as he replaced his bowler on his head. "I won't be but a moment."

Charlotte nodded and watched as Stewart retraced his steps, his stride upright and certain. She turned away, escaping to the side of the motorcar facing away from the church, and leaned her back against the door.

The pretense Charlotte had taken on became more difficult to maintain with each passing day. She was tired of living a lie; would she forever be entangled in a life of deceit? The thought wasn't comforting. When she had been with Eric, she had needed to do as he ordered, fearful of his wrath. But Eric wasn't here now.

Perhaps she should leave without telling anyone and find some kind of work in a nearby town. She was willing to learn a trade, as long as it wasn't her mother's. But then there was Michael.

Charlotte closed her eyes, realizing she was trapped in her sham. There was no escape without possibly causing harm to an innocent man. What would Michael do if she disappeared? Would he allow the guilt he harbored to tear at his soul again? Would he worry about her?

The crunch of footsteps on rocks brought her eyes open. A little girl, possibly seven or eight, stood a few feet away, her small hand gripping a bunch of wildflowers. Wide blue eyes stared up at Charlotte. A small blue hat covered brown braids that were tied with blue ribbons; she wore a white organdy dress. Her freckled face was unsmiling, and Charlotte stared back, uncertain of what to do or say.

The child took a few timid steps Charlotte's way, her wide-eyed gaze continuing to search Charlotte's. Charlotte had the uneasy feeling that the girl could see into her very soul, could discern her pain and all her tormenting secrets. She stopped in front of Charlotte, her head tilting back, her solemn gaze never wavering.

Charlotte dared not breathe as the seconds ticked by and some strange understanding seemed to pass between them. The child's lips tilted upward a fraction, and she held up the bouquet of buttercups and daisies.

With a shaky hand, Charlotte took the offering. "Thank you."

The girl nodded, then moved to go.

"Wait!"

She turned, the solemn expression again covering her face.

Charlotte floundered for something to say. "What's your name?"

The girl only stared at her for a moment with those strange, haunting eyes, then whirled around and hurried away, the wide blue bow at her waist bouncing with her quick steps.

Charlotte watched her go. After a moment, she dropped her gaze to the slightly drooping bouquet she held. Never had flowers looked more beautiful or smelled so sweet.

Stewart soon joined Myra, curious when he saw that she stood on the driver's side of the motorcar, staring at a bunch of wildflowers she held in one gloved hand.

"Planning to drive?" he asked with a grin.

"What?" She looked at him as if she'd just come out of a trance. "Drive? Oh." She glanced at the Tin Lizzy, her brow furrowing, as though just realizing her mistake.

"Where did you get the flowers? Did you pick them?"

"The flowers," she said softly with a wistful little smile, again staring at the bouquet. Her eyes lifted to his, and once more he was struck by their clear green color, reminding him of springtime. "A little girl brought them to me."

"A little girl? Did she have a name?" Stewart forced himself to look away from her face and took her elbow, walking her around to the other side of the car.

"She didn't tell me."

"Oh. Well, it was a sweet gesture."

Stewart shut her door, then went to the front of the car. He cupped his hand around the crank and brought it upward with a quick pull. The engine didn't catch. With a frustrated sigh, he repeated the process. This time the crank wrenched out of his hand, rotating with rapid speed, and the car backfired. He jerked his arm away to avoid a broken hand.

"Having trouble there, Stewart?" Doc Sanderson's jolly voice greeted him from behind. He turned and watched as the man waved from his buggy twenty feet away, one hand holding the reins to still his agitated horses. "If you ask Tom, I'm sure he'll let you buy back the carriage you traded in."

Stewart's mouth narrowed as he turned his back on the jovial doctor and waited for the engine to stop running backward. He pulled the crank upward with an angry jerk. The motor caught.

"Was there some trouble?" Myra asked as he took his place behind the wheel.

"Nothing I can't handle," Stewart muttered.

"Oh."

After several minutes of silence, Stewart realized he'd offended her. "How about a picnic? It's such a beautiful day."

She turned toward him, her creamy brow smoothing. "Yes, I think I'd like that."

"Excellent! We'll stop by my place, and I'll get Irma to prepare us something."

"Do you think Uncle Michael would mind?"

"I don't see why he would." He looked her way and saw worry furrow her brow again. "Michael needs rest, I'm certain, or he would've been at church this morning. He doesn't miss church unless he has to. My guess is, he'll take his lunch in his room."

"I suppose you're right. I just keep remembering what the doctor said, about how I need to be there for him more often."

Stewart reached across the space between them and covered her gloved hands with his. "You've been more than attentive these past three days, Myra. Michael told me your company has cheered him a great deal."

"I'm glad."

Stewart noticed that the expression on her face appeared more troubled than glad. A strong urge to comfort rose within him, and he wanted to enfold her in his arms.

Quickly he removed his hand from hers and placed it back on the wheel, uncomfortable with the unfamiliar feelings. He'd never met anyone who brought forth such emotions. Once, long before he became a Christian, he'd engaged in an illicit affair with a woman, but it soon soured, fortifying his decision never to marry. But Myra was different, seeming to be so lost and alone; she brought out a side of him he hadn't known existed.

Again he looked her way. He wished he could gain her confidence. If only she would trust him with whatever was bothering her. . . .

&

Charlotte stared out the window, almost wishing Stewart hadn't removed his hand. It had felt so warm and strong. She was coming to value his companionship and protection far too much, she realized. They could never be friends; there were too many secrets standing between them. And if he learned the truth. . . She couldn't stand to see him become her enemy.

"Here we are."

Charlotte looked with appreciation at the timbered, multistoried house nestled at the end of the lane, with cottonwoods for a backdrop. In the fenced-in pasture, a glossy black horse cantered. Though not as grand as Michael's place, Stewart's home was lovely and big. Dormer windows and two stone fireplaces added a touch of homeyness.

"Would you like to come inside?"

Charlotte shook her head, not willing to meet yet another curious stranger at the moment. "I'd prefer to wait out here if you don't mind."

"Of course." Stewart slid out of the car, then opened the door to the backseat and came around to Charlotte's side. "My secretary gave this to me yesterday. I'll make arrangements with Irma and be back as quickly as I can." He offered her a sympathetic parting look, then disappeared into the house.

Dread rose inside Charlotte as she fingered the two-week-old newspaper Stewart had laid in her lap. A long list of names was visible, and she briefly closed her eyes, summoning up courage.

The *Titanic's* survivors.

She carefully opened to the first page and began scanning the small print.

six

Stewart impatiently waited for Irma to tuck in the blanket she'd retrieved from the pantry. "Can't have the pretty miss ruin her dress, now can we? And would you care for some extra napkins, Mr. Lyons?" she asked, reaching for the linen cloths.

"No, that's fine, Irma," he said, grabbing the handle of the basket. He felt guilty to be gone so long, but Irma had been adamant that he wait until the cherry pie cool some before she packed it. He'd wanted to give Myra time alone to discover the truth about her friends, but he hadn't realized he would be gone this long.

His housekeeper fixed him with her stern brown gaze, her hands going to her ample hips. "And just when do I get to meet this young woman who has you all in a tizzy?"

"I'm not in a tizzy, Irma. I'm just trying to be friendly. You'll meet her soon."

Her dark brows arched upward. "Ah, 'friendly' he calls it. Well, it was called something else in my day, make no mistake about it," she said and laughed, turning away.

Stewart shook his head and hurried outside. When he caught sight of Myra, he reminded himself of his words to his housekeeper. Friendly, he was trying to be friendly. That's all. Nothing more.

His pounding heart mocked him.

Myra stared straight ahead, not even acknowledging him when he slipped behind the wheel after cranking the engine.

"You okay?" he asked.

She hesitated, then gave a swift nod.

"Bad news?"

"Yes. . .no." Her voice was whisper thin and barely audible above the rattling of the motorcar. "I'd rather not talk about it right now if you don't mind."

"I understand. If you'd rather I take you home—"

"No," she interrupted, her face turning his way. Her luminous eyes were pained but determined. "I want to go on the picnic."

"Then on a picnic we shall go," he said with a grin, hoping to elicit a smile from her. He failed.

Soon they reached the same clearing by the stream where they'd had their first picnic. He laid the blanket on the ground and spread out the bounty, making small talk all the while, and at times laughing like a fool—with no answering laughter in reply. Throwing his bowler aside, he said a blessing over the food, then stared at the roast beef sandwich and potato salad, no longer hungry.

Apparently Myra felt the same. Indeed, she seemed many miles away. . .in England? On the *Titanic*? What had put that frown on her rouged lips and that despair in her eyes?

He watched as she rose and took the few steps down the slope to the edge of the water. She looked at it for a long time, the breeze toying with her upswept hair and tugging at the hem of her dress. She was so beautiful, it took his breath away. And standing there as she did now, with the sun illuminating her and her hair afire with red light, she seemed too lovely to be real.

"Myra?" he asked, his voice coming out in a raspy breath that he was certain she couldn't hear above the splashing of the waterfall over the rocks.

She turned and walked along the waterline to a bush growing nearby. Small orange flowers covered it, and she reached toward one of the blossoms. "Oh!" She jerked her hand back.

Stewart shot to his feet and quickly reached her side. "What happened? Are you hurt?"

"It's nothing," she said, cupping one of her gloved hands to her chest.

He frowned. "Let me see."

"No, really, I—"

"Myra, give me your hand."

She hesitated, then reluctantly offered it to him. He gently took her left hand and turned it palm side up. A dot of red marred one of the white linen fingers.

"Take off your glove."

"I'm sure it's nothing."

Confused by her continued resistance, Stewart studied her face. Her cheeks were flushed, and panic lit her eyes.

"Myra, I won't hurt you. I promise. Now take off your glove." He turned to the stream, dipping his handkerchief in the water. When he again faced her, he noted with relief that the long glove was gone.

"Now let me see your hand," he coaxed.

Slowly she offered it to him. Her fingers were ice cold, but he was relieved to see the cut was minor. "You must have snagged it on a thorn or sharp twig." He moved his hand to circle her wrist and dabbed the wound gently. One side of her wrist seemed more pronounced than the other and, puzzled, he moved his fingers away until her small wrist lay cupped in his palm.

A sick feeling clenched his gut as he stared at her slim hand. His thumb gently brushed over the misshapen bump and the irregular white scar. Evidence of a healed break.

"How did this happen?" he asked, emotion choking his words. She tried to pull her hand away, but he tightened his grasp slightly. His gaze rose to meet hers. "Myra. . .did someone hurt you?"

Fear touched her eyes, followed by denial. "I don't know what you mean," she whispered. She looked so fragile, so vulnerable.

"Oh, Myra," he murmured, slowly pulling her into his embrace. His eyes closed as he rested his chin on her silken head, and his mouth moved against the fiery tresses. "When will you learn to trust me? What hidden pain do you carry that tortures you so?"

She stiffened, but he didn't remove his arms from around

her. His hands rubbed her tense shoulder blades, and after a few minutes of slow massage, he felt her muscles relax. She wilted against him, and her hands, trapped between them, tentatively moved beneath his jacket to circle his waist.

He inhaled swiftly, his mouth going dry. Lifting his head, he moved one hand to cup her chin with curled forefinger and thumb. She looked up at him, her green eyes a bit frightened but full of the same strong emotion that rocked him. Slowly, so as not to alarm her and give her every opportunity to pull back, he lowered his head to hers.

She didn't pull away.

Her mouth tasted of honey. Like a man who'd discovered buried treasure, he explored, tested, exulted in the soft contours of her lips. His hands moved to either side of her creamy face, gently cradling it. When her lips began to move over his, fire licked through his veins and he deepened the kiss—until a warning voice inside his head urged him to stop.

He pulled away, shaky and breathing heavily. Her half-closed eyes were glassy, and her rosy lips were still parted, as though begging him to continue. He almost gave in to the temptation but pulled back just in time, moving his chin to the top of her head, while keeping his arms protectively around her.

"I've come to care for you a great deal, Myra," he said, his voice husky. "In fact, I highly suspect I've fallen in love with you."

Stewart's soft words broke through Charlotte's muddled senses like a stone hurled into a peaceful pond. She pushed against his chest, taking a quick step backward.

His brow furrowed. "Myra?"

"No." She shook her head, taking a few more steps in reverse when he took a step toward her. "Don't love me, Stewart. I'm not worth it."

"What do you mean you're not worth it? You're talking nonsense."

She bit back the tide of rising tears, lifting her chin in an attempt to stay in control. "I'm not the woman you think I am. I would only ruin your life. Forget about me."

Turning away from the stunned bewilderment in his eyes, she hurried up the slope toward the forgotten picnic. Stewart's kiss had awakened something dormant inside of her. Never had she been kissed in such a way. Eric's rare kisses had been selfish. . .possessive. But Stewart left her feeling cherished.

She closed her eyes, her nails biting into her palms. Eric. She could scarcely believe he was dead, though the list had proven it. Yet that didn't change her present circumstances. For a brief time, in Stewart's arms, she'd forgotten who she was and why a relationship between them couldn't be possible.

She would never forget again.

She heard him come up behind her and stiffened. "I think I should go back to my uncle's now."

There was a pause. "Myra, look at me."

Reluctant, she slowly turned and stared at the third button of his tweed jacket.

"I don't understand why you feel the way you do, but I won't push you." His hand went beneath her chin, forcing her gaze to meet his. His hazel eyes glowed with determination. "However, be warned. I've rarely lost a case in my three years as an attorney, and I don't intend to lose now. You're very special, Myra Flannigan, and I shall do all within my power to prove it to you. Even if it means waiting an extended amount of time until you're ready to open your heart to me."

"Stewart, I—"

He put two fingers to her lips to ward off her coming argument. "Shhh. Not a word. From your response to my kiss I think you care for me, too. But as I told you, I won't push."

She gave a helpless shrug, lowering her gaze, and he turned to gather the uneaten food into the picnic basket.

The ride home was devoid of conversation. When he pulled up in front of Larkin's Glen, he grabbed the basket and handed it to her. "It would be a shame to let all this good food go to waste. Take it. You and Michael can have a picnic in his room. I need to be getting home now."

She took the basket, trying to think of something to say. "I'm sorry," she finally croaked in a voice barely heard over the engine's racket.

"You've nothing to be sorry about." He gave her an encouraging grin. "I'll be back, Myra. You're not rid of me so easily."

Her traitorous heart leapt for joy at his words. She offered an uncertain smile, then hurried away.

❧

Eyeing Charlotte, Michael finished his roast beef sandwich. "What ails ye, Lass? You've been quiet since you came up to visit me. Did you and Stewart have a row? Is that why you came home so early?"

She shrugged, forcing herself to eat a bite of potato salad.

"He fancies you, you know. I've seen the way he makes eyes at you."

Heat flamed her cheeks. "I know."

"He's a good man, he is. You couldn't do better than Stewart Lyons."

"It's not that," Charlotte said, desperately wanting to change the subject.

"Are you homesick for England then?"

She laid down her fork, giving up all pretense of trying to eat. "Not really. There are too many sad memories for me there."

"In time the sadness will fade, and you'll remember only the happy times, Lass." Michael shook his head. "Your stepfather was a good man. Ma and Da should never have done what they did to Katie."

Charlotte sat very still, afraid to say anything and reveal her ignorance concerning the situation.

"Aye, Angus Flannigan was also a good man, but he was a fighter. And as hot-blooded as they come. When your da was killed in a riot in Ireland and Katie came to the States, expecting you, we tried to console her as best we could. But

Charles. . .well, Charles seemed to be the only one who could reach her, and I could see the love between them a-bloomin'. When she defied our parents by marrying a Brit and going to his home in England. . ." Michael sighed. " 'Twas a hard thing when they disowned her, to be sure. A hard thing. . ."

Sadness clouded his eyes. "I visited her that summer, a month after you were born, though my parents were none too happy aboot it. But I couldn't abandon Katie, as they had done."

"Was that the only time you visited England?"

"Aye. The only time." The lines in his face deepened and remorse filled his eyes. He shook his head and looked away. "I'm feeling a wee bit tired, Lass. I tank I'll rest a spell." His brogue thickened as it always did when he was upset.

Concern filled her. "Are you all right?"

"Aye, nothing to alarm yourself aboot. However, if you've a mind, could you read me a chapter or two from the Bible? I've missed the church meetings."

Charlotte bit the inside of her lip, looking toward the black book sitting on a side table. "If you'd like," she said hesitantly.

Michael settled among the pillows, closing his eyes, and Charlotte opened to the place where the frayed ribbon marked the page. She cleared her throat and began to read from the Gospel of John.

❧

Charlotte's slapping footsteps echoed off the ramshackle buildings closing her in on both sides of the long alleyway. Swirls of thick mist reached out gray tendril-like fingers, seeking to capture her. She knew that if she stopped running, they would win and draw her into their clammy world—forever cutting her off from the light. Yet she could never quite reach the light at the end of the alley, no matter how fast she ran on her swollen bare feet. The light grew brighter, and, hopeful, she drew on another burst of speed, her white nightgown billowing around her ankles. A hand shot out of a doorway and grabbed her wrist. She screamed and turned to wrest herself away—and came face to face with a leering Eric.

"No!" she cried, but he only threw back his head and laughed, his hold on her tightening, until she felt bones crunching. He drew her close, closer. . .then his face changed, and she was looking at Stewart. He shook his head, his eyes sad, his mouth forming the soundless word "guilty." He shoved her away and let her go. Screaming in terror, Charlotte fell headlong into a black abyss, the sound of a jail door clanging behind her. Loud knocking permeated the thick darkness that smothered her and tried to take away her last breath.

Charlotte bolted upright in bed, her heart beating fast and her body drenched with sweat. Her wide-eyed gaze roamed the familiar oak furnishings of the room bathed in sunlight. Relieved to discover it had only been another of the many nightmares she'd had since her arrival at Larkin's Glen, she settled back against the pillows with a sigh.

A knock thudded against her door, and from the impatient sound of it, Charlotte surmised that this hadn't been her first summons.

Quickly she slid out of bed, donned her woolen wrapper, and cinched it tight. Opening the door a crack, she saw Mrs. Manning on the threshold. "Yes?"

"You have a visitor, Miss Flannigan."

"A visitor? You mean Mr. Lyons?" What was he doing here this time of morning? She'd slept later than usual, certainly, but he never came 'til midafternoon or later, when he did visit.

"No, Miss. A lady visitor."

"A lady?" The cold in the room seemed to creep into her every pore and freeze her blood. "A neighbor of my uncle's?"

Mrs. Manning's eyes narrowed. "No, not a neighbor. She mentioned sailing on the *Titanic*. Said her maid Sadie bought a baby blanket you'd crocheted, and she wants to talk to you about helping to set up a business. Odd time to come visiting if you ask me, but she said this was the only time she may be this way again. She gave me this to give to you."

Curious, Charlotte looked down at the calling card the housekeeper placed in her hand. Chills traveled down her spine, and her grip on the ivory parchment tightened as she read the name in fancy black script: *Lady Annabelle Caldwell.*

Charlotte's day of reckoning had come.

seven

Charlotte gripped the bundle tighter as she approached the front parlor. She turned to Mrs. Manning, who lingered close by. "I don't wish to be disturbed."

The housekeeper's gray brows lifted to her hairline, but she gave a deferential nod. "As you wish, Miss."

Taking a deep breath while gathering her courage, Charlotte opened the door, swept inside, then closed the door softly behind her.

Annabelle stood staring at a painting above the mantel, her back to Charlotte. At the door's click, she turned, a pleasant smile of greeting on her smooth face. Her emerald eyes widened, the smile slowly fading.

"Mademoiselle Fontaneau," she said, as though in a stupor. "I thought you were dead. But. . .what are you doing here? I came to see Myra Flannigan."

Charlotte gave a slight nod, wishing she could still the beating of her wildly racing heart. "Miss Mooreland—or should I say Lady Caldwell. I understand congratulations are in order."

Suspicion replaced the shock on Annabelle's face. "So, you're no longer French, I see. I must say, your British accent sounds much more convincing."

Charlotte bit the inside of her lip, then gave a stiff nod. "I was born in London and lived my entire life there."

Puzzlement drew Annabelle's dark brows together. "Then why. . .?"

Charlotte left her post by the door and strode across the room. She stopped in front of Annabelle and held out the bulky kerchief. "Perhaps this might help explain things."

Annabelle shook her head, uncomprehending, but took the

bundle and opened it. She gasped as the sparkling jewels spilled into her hands. "My mother's diamonds," she whispered. She turned wide eyes to Charlotte. "But I thought they went down with the *Titanic*. How did you get them?"

Charlotte bent to retrieve the paper that had fluttered to the floor at Annabelle's feet and laid it in the brunette's cold hands. "And the deed to your house."

Annabelle blinked at the paper and the diamonds, then her gaze again went to Charlotte. "I don't understand. . . ."

"You were right not to like me," Charlotte said, her voice wavering. "The day I invited you to talk with me in my cabin, Eric was in your stateroom, stealing the diamonds from your safe. My job was to divert you and give him the time he needed to finish the deed."

If possible, Annabelle's eyes widened even further.

"I also was responsible for putting a drug into your father's drink to make him forgetful and to assure that Eric would win the card game. But I had no idea Eric's greed would cause him to stoop to accepting the stakes of your house."

Frowning, Annabelle sank onto the stuffed chair behind her. "Why are you telling me this? Why now? And—and where is Myra Flannigan? What have you done with her?"

"Myra died in the sinking." At the memory, Charlotte crossed her arms tightly against her chest and clasped her elbows. "I saw her body in the ocean."

"Then if she's dead. . .why are you here?" Annabelle's eyes narrowed with suspicion.

Uncertain how much she should reveal, Charlotte took a few steps away from Annabelle and stood staring at the cold fireplace, then again turned to face the woman she'd wronged. "Eric wasn't my brother. I was his cohort for three years, and. . .and I assisted him in his thievery. I assumed Myra's identity after the sinking because I was afraid he might look for me."

Anger flashed in Annabelle's eyes. "I see. . . ."

"No, Lady Caldwell, you don't," Charlotte said grimly. "You

could never know what I was forced to endure, though I realize that's no excuse for my behavior. Please believe me now when I say I mean no harm in this present pretense. I don't want Michael Larkin's money. I only want to find peace."

"Michael Larkin?"

"Myra's uncle."

Annabelle's mouth narrowed. "And why should I believe you, Charlotte? How do I know this isn't another one of your tricks? That you're not deceiving me as you did my father!"

"You don't know, that's true. And I can't fault you for being suspicious. But keep in mind that I didn't have to come down here. I could have told Mrs. Manning to send you away, that I didn't feel like receiving visitors, and you would have never been the wiser. Nor did I have to give you back the jewelry or the deed. You never even guessed the jewels had been stolen. I knew that. By returning your things to you, surely that proves I'm trying to make amends the only way I know how."

Annabelle gave a grudging nod, then looked down at the crumpled paper in her hand. "Strange, but this doesn't mean as much to me as it once did," she said slowly, as though speaking to herself. "Lawrence must go back to England soon, and I and Peter with him. But I don't ever want to set foot on a ship after that. Perhaps I will give the house to my aunt. . . ."

"Is Peter the little boy who was on the stretcher?" Charlotte asked, breaking into Annabelle's musings. "I saw the picture of the three of you in the newspaper."

Annabelle lifted her gaze to Charlotte, her brow furrowed. "Picture? I saw no picture, though I know reporters were there when we disembarked and made our way to the ambulance. Lawrence saved Peter's life aboard the *Titanic*. We are in the process of adopting him."

"I see."

An uncomfortable span of silence ensued, and Annabelle shifted. "I'm in a quandary concerning all you've told me. I cannot leave here in good conscience, knowing about your lie to Myra's uncle—and do nothing about it."

Charlotte bit the inside of her lip, rubbing her hands over her arms. "Once I discovered for certain that Eric had died in the sinking, it was my plan to tell Mr. Larkin the truth, perhaps find employment in a nearby town. . . ."

Annabelle nodded. "That sounds like a good plan."

"Yes, but there's a problem." Charlotte sighed and sank into the chair opposite Annabelle's. "Mr. Larkin is under medical care. I had a consultation with his doctor, and he informed me that my being here is just what Michael needs. If I were to tell him the truth, it might damage his health further. I could never live with the knowledge that I was responsible for such a thing. I'm not as heartless as you think me."

Annabelle's brows drew downward. "But is it fair to let Mr. Larkin believe you're his relation when you're not?"

"He's a widower and childless. I—or rather, Myra—am the only relation he has left, or so he believes."

"A difficult state of affairs, for certain," Annabelle soberly agreed. "But living a lie will only make it worse."

"I know." How well she knew. The peace that Charlotte had sought since arriving at Larkin's Glen had eluded her. "Yet keep in mind, Lady Caldwell, that this doesn't only concern my future. It concerns Mr. Larkin's health and peace of mind as well."

Annabelle was silent a moment, thoughtful. "I don't know exactly what kind of life you formerly led with Eric, nor do I wish to know. However, considering the past few minutes, I can see that you do indeed have a heart to change. I sense your sincerity, and I don't suspect you've a hidden motive in your pretense of Myra—though I certainly don't agree with your charade. . . ."

Annabelle took her time putting the jewelry and deed into her reticule, and Charlotte thought she might expire from the suspense.

"Very well, Charlotte. Given the unusual circumstances, I

will keep your secret—though I still don't feel right about this. Deceit is never the answer."

"Yes, I know. Thank you," Charlotte said in relief.

Annabelle hesitated. "Have you given any thought to our previous discussion about God?"

"Many times. I've even attended church."

Surprise touched Annabelle's features, and she smiled for the first time since seeing Charlotte. "I can't tell you how pleased I am to hear that. Jesus is the answer to all your problems, Charlotte. He will give you the solution you seek."

Charlotte didn't respond, and Annabelle rose.

"I must be going. I'm supposed to be on a shopping spree. Good afternoon." She stopped once she reached the door and turned, her eyes serious again. "Please give some thought about being honest with Mr. Larkin. I know it's a difficult situation for all involved, but truth is always the best way. God can work things out."

Charlotte gave a grudging nod.

Annabelle hesitated, then smiled. "I'm glad you survived."

Surprise filled Charlotte but soon faded when she realized the meaning behind Annabelle's words. "Because of the return of your jewels and the deed, of course."

"No, Charlotte. Because of you. I'm glad you didn't die."

Charlotte looked away, uncomfortable. No one had ever cared about her welfare before, besides her mother—in her own mixed-up way. "And your father?" she asked softly.

"He was lost at sea."

"I'm sorry."

"He was happy to go, and that gives me peace. Good-bye, Charlotte. I shall keep you in my prayers."

After Annabelle left, Charlotte sought the solace of the garden, mingled feelings of confusion and relief warring within her. She felt a tad lighter, as if a weight had been lifted now that she'd returned Annabelle's things to their rightful owner. If only she could be honest with Michael Larkin. But she just didn't see how such a thing was possible.

2a

"Are you all right? You seem troubled."

Stewart's soft voice broke into Charlotte's thoughts, and she looked up from watching the blades of grass sail down the stream. "I'm a bit confused."

"Confused?"

"I didn't understand the minister's message today."

"Ah." Stewart propped his bended arm on his upraised knee. "Something about St. Paul's conversion confuses you?"

"Yes." Charlotte plucked up another handful of grass and threw it into the moving stream. "After he was responsible for so many deaths of God's people, how could God choose him to spread His gospel?"

Stewart grinned, his eyes twinkling. "Ah, but Myra, the Bible is full of such cases. Murderers, prostitutes, liars and thieves—God calls them all to repentance and a life with Him."

"But that doesn't make any sense." She straightened, wrapped her arms around her knees, and fixed him with a puzzled stare. "When there are so many good people on the earth, why would God pick the bad to do His work?"

"Good people on the earth?" Stewart shook his head. "Remember what Christ told the man who called Him good in last week's message? That there is not one who is good—only the Father who abides in heaven."

"Well, that doesn't make sense either," she argued. "Since Christ was God, then He was good. So why should He tell that man otherwise?"

"I suppose it's because the man didn't know that he was speaking to God in the flesh. Jesus hadn't yet revealed Himself to the people. By His statement, I believe He was telling us that in God's eyes, everyone falls short of the mark. Everyone needs to accept Christ to enter the kingdom of heaven."

"I suppose. . . ."

Stewart's brows drew down. "Myra, you've made that choice, haven't you? I'd assumed from what Michael told me. . ."

She broke eye contact. "I've done a lot of wrong things in my life, Stewart. Things I'm not proud of."

"That's one of the reasons Jesus died on the cross. To take your sins upon Him. He ate and talked with sinners because He knew they needed His teachings the most."

"I . . ." She bit her lip and continued to stare at the ground, tears blurring her eyes. "I still don't understand why He would die for me, though, when I've done nothing for Him."

"Because He loves you, Myra. Don't try to understand God, just accept His free gift to you: the gift of salvation."

She gave a slight nod, a flicker of a smile on her lips.

"Come here." His voice was gruff, and Charlotte glanced up, suddenly alarmed.

"Don't look at me like that, little one. Don't you know yet that I would never hurt you?"

The temptation of his open arms was too great, and Charlotte went to him, letting him enfold her in his warmth and protection. He pulled her onto his lap, holding her close, and gently rocked her until she felt the tears dry. She gazed over his shoulder at the trees lining the stream, at the shallow water rushing over the rocks, and she relaxed.

Stewart's warm mouth touched her temple, and Charlotte raised her head, her eyes questioning. He searched her face, his gaze roaming each feature. To her surprise, he pulled his kerchief from his pocket and, with one corner of the white cloth over his index finger, reached over and dipped it in the water. He brought the cloth to her lips and gently dabbed at them.

"You're much too beautiful for paint, little one."

Charlotte stared in shock as the bold color on her mouth transferred to the kerchief. Eric had insisted she wear paint, complaining her looks too plain without it. And Stewart thought her beautiful?

"There," he said in a satisfied tone, pocketing the kerchief again. "Much better."

She blinked, not knowing what to say. He continued to stare at her. Lifting his hand, he cupped her face and brushed the pad of his thumb over her lower lip. She felt him tremble, then his lips touched hers in a soft kiss, as brief as a butterfly's landing.

The strange consuming heat she'd lately experienced when she was in Stewart's arms flooded Charlotte, but before she could respond to his kiss, he pulled away and offered a shaky smile.

"I suppose we should pack up the picnic leavings, and I should return you to your uncle. We've been here for more than an hour."

She nodded, feeling a bit snubbed by his sudden withdrawal, though she had no right to enjoy his kisses. But she did, very much. He made her feel cherished. And when she was in his arms, she never wanted to leave them.

Stewart gently pushed her from his lap to a standing position. He rose from the ground and began cleaning up the picnic site. Then they silently made their way to the motorcar.

❧

An old woman with straggly white hair and few teeth in her head beckoned from her place on the park bench. "Come 'ere, little flower girl. Come 'ere—I won't bite ye."

Charleigh clutched the stems of the posies tighter in one hand and shuffled to the bench.

"What's yer name?" the old woman asked, her faded blue eyes crinkling at the corners, her chapped lips turning upward in a smile.

"Charleigh, Mum." She gulped. "Would ye. . .would ye like to buy a flower?"

Regret filled the woman's eyes. "Sorry, Luv, I 'aven't a pence to me name."

"Oh." Charleigh turned to go, then stopped. The woman looked hungry, and Charleigh knew what hunger felt like. It made her stomach hurt. Like it did now.

She bit her lip, uncertain, then slipped a grubby hand into the frayed pocket of her sweater and pulled out the sixpence she'd earned that morning from a generous customer. She turned and held it out to the woman. " 'Ere, Mum. To buy a hot bun." Giles, the mean man who owned the tavern, would be angry, and her mum might be mad, too. But Charleigh would work harder to earn back the missing money.

Tears filled the woman's eyes as she stared at the silver coin shining dully in Charleigh's dirty little palm. She lifted her head. "How old are ye, Luv?"

"Six."

"An' where's your mum, Child?"

"She works at the tavern."

A very sad look filled the woman's eyes. "An' your papa?"

"I don't 'ave a papa."

The old woman shook her head. "Then ye best had keep that, Charleigh. Your mum needs it. I may not 'ave much to me name, but I do 'ave the Lord." She smiled again. "Yer a good girl. An' I want ye to know that as long as the good Lord sees fit to keep me alive, I will pray for ye. Every day."

❧

Memory of that forgotten afternoon brought Charlotte's eyes wide, and she stopped weeding her little plot in the garden. It had been so long ago, yet she remembered the event with such clarity. She'd only seen the old woman twice after that, and she told her the same thing each time. That she would pray for her.

And she had. She had told Charlotte who God was, and that innocent six-year-old child had prayed with the woman, asking Jesus to come live inside her heart.

But God could never want her now.

A painful lump lodged in Charlotte's throat as she stared down at the flower bed and the dirt caked on her fingers. She dusted off her hands, then wiped them on the apron Tildy had lent her to protect her dress. Brown still colored the creases of her palms and remained underneath her nails.

You're like that dirt, the cruel voice whispered inside her head. *No matter what you try to do to rid yourself of it and make yourself clean, it will never happen. The dirt will always remain.*

Charlotte wiped her hands harder on the apron until her palms burned from the friction. Again she looked. The dirt was still there.

Tears blurred her vision, and she sank from her kneeling position onto her legs. Her gaze lifted to the blooming roses trailing a vine up the white picket fence, but she only saw bright pink splotches among the green against a shimmering white background. She swiped a curled forefinger under her eyes to clear her vision.

Come unto me, a softer and more calm voice whispered, *all ye that labour and are heavy laden, and I will give you rest.*

Charlotte sat still, her brow furrowing as the Scripture Michael had read aloud two days ago during their daily Bible time filled her mind. She concentrated, closing her eyes. How did the rest of it go?

Take my yoke upon you, and learn of me; for I am meek and lowly in heart: and ye shall find rest unto your souls. For my yoke is easy, and my burden is light.

Charlotte's eyes opened wide as the verse lit her mind like a sudden bright sunbeam. Then just as quickly, it faded, when she realized she could never be worthy of such love.

She lowered her head, allowing several tears to splash on her hands balled in her lap. "I can never be good enough, Lord. You could never want me now. Not after all I've done. . . ."

Another forgotten memory flew through her mind. A dark closet. . .the sour smell of ale and the sound of rodents scurrying within the peeling walls. . . . Charlotte as a small child, huddled up in one corner, her thin arms tightly clasped around her upraised knees, hot tears trailing down her dirty face. Repeated smacks of a fist viciously hitting skin sounded in the next room. . .followed by her mother's pain-filled cries.

"Dear Jesus, make him stop hurting my mum," she had whispered into her wool skirt. "I'll be a good girl, only please make him stop hurting her. Please. . . ."

The evil man stopped, growled a few foul words, and left.

Charleigh crawled out of the closet, afraid. Her mother lay beaten and bloody on the cot, and Charleigh forced back her fear and hurried to get a cloth and some water from the pitcher.

As she tended her mum with shaking hands, the woman opened her eyes and looked upon her daughter. "Charleigh," she said in a hoarse, shaky voice. "I promise you'll never go through this. If I have to kill or steal, I'll make certain that you don't end up like me. . . ."

"Oh, Mum!" Charlotte wailed now as she slumped over, putting her dirt-stained hands to her face. Her body convulsed with broken sobs, though this time the pain was too deep for tears. "Why did you sell me to Eric? Why?! Did you honestly think that would be a better fate for me than the life you led? He lied, Mum. . .he lied to you and me both! The night the *Titanic* sank, he told me—"

A snapping twig brought Charlotte's head around. Dread swamped her, and it seemed as if all the blood drained from her body and into the ground where she sat.

Stewart stood a few feet away, his eyes wide with shock.

eight

"Myra, what's wrong?" Stewart quickly covered the distance between them and squatted in front of her.

She stared, her green eyes large and frantic, her face wet with tears. Her hands clutched the grass on either side, as if to anchor her and keep her from falling. "How. . .how long have you been there?" Her pain-wracked voice was barely above a whisper.

"I just arrived."

He couldn't miss the relief that lit her eyes, but almost immediately it was gone, and a shutter seemed to close over them.

"Is it Michael? Has something happened to your uncle?"

"No, no. He's fine."

"Then why were you—"

"I'm fine." She stood, not asking for assistance, and brushed the soil from the apron tied around her waist. All expression was gone from her face, which now looked bland. "I need to retire to my room now. If you'll excuse me. . . ."

Stunned by the lightning-fast change in her, Stewart tried to collect his thoughts and make order of what had just happened. Except for the wetness on her cheeks, there was no evidence of what had just taken place. And what exactly had taken place? Stewart wished he knew. The one thing he'd heard her say, about someone lying to both her and her mother, only heightened his curiosity to know more.

"Myra, wait!" he called out before she reached the door, remembering the reason he'd come. "I thought you might like to take a drive with me. I bought back my horse and buggy. . . ."

She didn't turn around. "Not today, Stewart. I need to go lie down. I'm feeling rather tired."

"All right." He ran a frustrated hand over the back of his

neck. Why wouldn't she look at him? "Then I'll pick you up for church tomorrow?"

She hesitated, then gave a slight nod before hurrying into the house.

Stewart had no idea how long he stared at the closed door, but when he heard a deep chuckle, he whipped his head sideways.

"Top o' the mornin' to ye, me boy." Michael's eyes twinkled and a grin covered his ruddy face as he sauntered toward him. "Would ye be of a mind to tell me what you are doing down there? Inspecting ant hills, perhaps?"

Stewart looked from Michael to the grass, realizing he was still squatting before the flower bed, one hand braced on the ground. Embarrassed, he shot to a standing position and smoothed his pants before looking at Michael again.

The grin was still plastered on his face.

"I was talking with Myra," Stewart explained, feeling more than a little ridiculous.

His bushy brows lifting toward his hairline, Michael looked at the empty air beside Stewart. "Myra. . .?" Amusement laced his voice.

"Well, she was here a moment ago."

Michael bellowed a laugh. "And were you proposing, to be down on your knees like that? Did you scare her away, Lad?"

Stewart felt heat surge up his neckline and tugged at his collar. It was time to change the subject. Fast.

"Will you be joining us for church tomorrow, Michael?" he asked gruffly. "I bought back my old buggy."

"Now there's a piece of good news!" The older man's smile widened. "I would ken even Myra would appreciate the change in transportation. Is that what you were doing? On your knees begging her to go riding with you?"

There was no talking to Michael when he was like this.

"I'll be leaving now," Stewart muttered. He stopped as an idea struck. He turned around. "I need to go to Manhattan this week, on business. I could take Myra with me to do some shopping if you'd like. There are some very nice boutiques and department stores in the area."

For the first time Michael grew solemn. "Aye, the lass does need clothes for certain. I've been remiss not to attend to it sooner. You've me permission to take her, Stewart, but you'd best check with Myra and see if she's beholdin' to the idea as well." The twinkle was back in his eye.

Stewart pushed his hat further down on his head and strode out the gate to the front of the house. Was it obvious to everyone how deep his feelings went for her? First Irma, now Michael. Stewart shook his head, climbed into his buggy, and took the reins. He looked back at the house one last time.

Myra stood at an upper window, clutching the curtains to the side, staring down at him. Stewart's breath caught in his throat as he lifted a hand in farewell. She hesitated, slowly lifting her hand. Then she was gone.

Stewart stared at the opaque curtains, which had moved back into place. How could he ever get past the barrier she'd placed between them? But more important, why had she put it there?

❧

Charlotte spent the rest of the afternoon in her room. When dinnertime came, she joined Michael at the long dining table, though she felt little like eating. Still, she enjoyed his company. He was more talkative than usual, and Charlotte was relieved to see a marked improvement in his outward appearance and appetite as well.

Afterward, they sat in the garden, as was their daily custom, and by the sun's last light continued their Bible readings. But tonight Charlotte's mind was on other things.

"I have a question," she said, fidgeting with a loose thread in her skirt. "Why is the painting in the parlor called *In the Secret Place*? I've often wondered."

Michael closed the book and set it on the bench beside him. He looked at her thoughtfully. "This is where Anna took her morning devotions. She said the beauty of God's handiwork satisfied her soul, while God's Word filled her spirit."

"So it was her secret place to meet with God?"

He thought awhile, then nodded. "She based the name of the place on the first verses in Psalm 91: 'He that dwelleth in the secret place of the most High shall abide under the shadow of the Almighty. I will say of the LORD, He is my refuge and my fortress: my God; in him will I trust.' "

The words sent shivers down Charlotte's spine.

"Anna couldn't have children," he continued sadly. "A debilitating disease took away her ability to do so, taking her life in the end."

"Oh," Charlotte breathed in surprise.

Michael nodded. "She was a woman of courage. I once asked her how she could be so strong when she had not an ounce of physical strength. Do you know what she told me?"

Charlotte shook her head, though he wasn't looking at her.

"She said that it's only through her time with God in the secret place that she developed the strength she needed to go on each day. Without that time, she said she probably would have given up long ago." He closed his eyes at the memory.

Charlotte bit the inside corner of her lip, her gaze drifting down to her lap. "She sounds as if she was a good woman. Someone God would want to talk to."

"She had faith, she did. It was her strong faith and God's mercy that kept us together," he murmured, as if to himself.

Charlotte looked up in surprise. "There was trouble between you?" As soon as the words left her mouth, Charlotte realized how rude and intrusive they were. She was about to apologize, when he spoke.

"There was an. . .incident in my youth that almost tore us apart when it came to light." The lines in his face became more pronounced. "For weeks Anna would not speak to me. Only God in His mercy salvaged our marriage."

Charlotte didn't know what to say, so she remained quiet.

"Ach, but the past is past, as me mother used to say. No use bringing it up." He shook his head and smiled, though his eyes were still sad. "I think I'll turn in for the night, Lass. I'm a mite tired, and I really want to attend church in the morning. Good night."

"Sleep well." Drawing her brows together in concern, Charlotte watched as he shuffled to the house with bowed shoulders. If she knew how to pray, she would ask God to take away Michael's sorrow, for obviously he still carried the burden of his past. A man such as Michael didn't deserve such penance.

She cast a tentative, curious glance at the Bible he'd left on the bench. Biting her lip, she grabbed the thick book in trembling fingers, spread it open in her lap, and by the dying light of the sun, found and read Psalm 91.

&

The morning air was cool and crisp as Charlotte exited the church, Michael on one side of her, Stewart on the other. Stewart was called away by a panicked young man, and a bevy of tongue-clucking middle-aged women converged on Michael—fretting and fawning over him, telling him that if he had a good woman to care for him, there would be no need for doctors.

Michael sent Charlotte a silent plea for help, but she only smiled, ignoring the desperate look in his eyes, because she'd seen the grin tilting his lips. Michael, for all his silent protestations, was enjoying the attention of these women, who were obviously vying to be the next Mrs. Larkin. And why not? Michael was a fine figure of a man, with a heart of gold to match.

Charlotte listened in amusement as the widowed Mrs. Boswell assured Michael that she was the finest cook in the state and she could make an Irish stew that would have him begging for more. As she talked, the feathers on her hat swayed with the motion of her head, bobbing up and down. Charlotte put her hand to her mouth, stifling a laugh, when she saw Michael's blue gaze following the fluttering feathers.

Before getting herself into trouble, Charlotte made her

escape. Seeing Stewart still in conversation with the young man, she walked around the side of the church, where she'd seen some children running alongside the same spotted dog Charlotte had seen her first day there. A cemetery stood at the back, catty-corner to the church. Sobering, Charlotte picked her way over the dewy grass and yellow wildflowers to read the engraved headstones.

Here lies my beloved Hazel. Taken in youth, a blooming flower never to fade. 1852–1869

Charlotte crossed her arms tightly against her, grasping her elbows. Oh, to be loved like that. To be loved at all. . .

"Papa and Mama went to heaven, too," a hollow, weak voice said near Charlotte's elbow.

Charlotte turned in surprise. The little girl who'd given her the flowers stood in the same dress and bonnet, looking at Charlotte with the same haunting blue eyes. The past few Sundays the child had been absent, and Charlotte had begun to wonder if she'd imagined her. Yet the wildflowers on her vanity, now shriveled and brown, assured her daily that the experience had been real.

"Did your mama and papa die?" the little girl asked.

Emotion clutched Charlotte's throat. "My mum did. I never knew my papa."

The girl solemnly nodded and slipped her hand into Charlotte's gloved one, turning to stare at the granite headstone. Charlotte looked down at the bonneted head, her heart twisting at the child's vulnerability and pain. Together they stared at the gray stone, hands clasped, and shared the common bond of sorrow.

"Amanda?" a woman's incredulous voice called from behind them.

The girl turned, as did Charlotte. A young woman stood staring at the two, open-mouthed, her light blue eyes going from one to the other and then to their clasped hands. Like the child, she was dressed expensively and wore a peach silk dress with narrow black pinstripes and black hat adorned with beige feathers and orange ribbons. Only the lines of strain between her dark brows and alongside her mouth gave evidence to the trials she must carry.

"Amanda, I've been looking for you everywhere," the woman said softly, though Charlotte noticed she spoke with great care, as though uncertain of the girl's reaction. "We need to get on home now. Go on to the buggy, Dear."

Amanda gave a swift nod, letting her hand fall away from Charlotte's. She gave Charlotte one last look. A smile softly tilted the corners of her mouth. "Good-bye."

"Good-bye," Charlotte said, returning the smile.

She watched as the girl strode away, the blue ribbons on her hat and dress billowing in the gentle breeze. The woman hadn't moved, and, curious, Charlotte turned toward her.

Complete shock covered her features, her eyes wide as she watched Amanda turn the corner at the front of the church. She continued to stare at the empty spot, then turned dazed eyes to Charlotte. "She spoke to you." Her voice was hoarse.

Hoping the child wasn't in trouble, Charlotte gave a slight shrug. "She didn't say much. She came while I was looking at the headstone and mentioned that her parents are dead."

Tears filled the woman's eyes. "But you don't understand," she countered, emotion clouding her voice and making it difficult for her to talk. "Amanda hasn't spoken to anyone for months, ever since her parents—my sister and her husband— died in a fire. She hasn't said a word in all that time. . . ."

Tears spilled over her lower lashes and down her cheeks. "Not until today, that is."

"I had no idea. . . ," was all Charlotte could think to say.

The woman acted as if she could hold back no longer and smothered Charlotte in a hearty hug. "Oh, thank you!" she said. "I don't know what you did or how you did it—but thank you for being here, for helping Amanda come out of her shell."

"But really, I didn't do a thing," Charlotte protested.

The woman pulled away, her slim hands going to Charlotte's shoulders, her head cocking a fraction to the side as she studied her with earnestness. "God used you, I'm sure of it. No one's had any success with Amanda up until now. God used you to bring my niece back to me."

Her words mocked Charlotte. God used her? The idea was ludicrous. Why would God want anything to do with her when there were so many good people to choose from?

Again the Scripture she'd heard that morning from Romans filtered through her mind. "There are none good, no not one. . . for all have sinned and come short of the glory of God."

"Myra?"

Stewart's questioning tone brought Charlotte's head around. He stood about twenty feet away, his dark eyebrows lifted, curious yet obviously not wishing to intrude. The woman dropped her hands from Charlotte's shoulders.

"I should let you go now," she said, dashing the tears from her face. "I'm so glad Stewart found someone like you. Several tried to gain his attention, but failed every time. My husband and I—and half the town, I'm sure—wondered if he'd ever marry." She grinned conspiratorially, and Charlotte felt her face flush.

"You're a peach, Miss Flannigan. I can never thank you enough for what you've done. Please come and visit us soon. We live about a mile and a half up the road. I would love to cook you Sunday dinner sometime." And with another quick hug, she waved to Stewart and was gone.

Stewart walked up to Charlotte, who still felt numb from the experience. "I must say," he murmured, amusement lacing his voice, "that's the most lively I've seen Lucy Porter in a long time. Whatever did you say to her?"

Charlotte shook her head. "I really don't understand. . . . She thinks I'm responsible for getting her niece to talk. . . ."

"Amanda spoke?" he asked, turning to her with an incredulous stare. "Really?"

Charlotte attempted a smile. "Yes."

"Well, I'll be. . ." He stared after the Porters' departing buggy. "That child hasn't said a word since her parents died eight months ago in a fire. They were vacationing in Paris at the time, and the hotel where they stayed burned. I took care of legal matters afterward. Lucy and Jake asked me then if I thought they should get help for Amanda. I've known the Porters since we were children. . . ."

His words trailed off, and he looked back at Charlotte, shaking his head in wonder. His eyes were full of admiration.

She fidgeted and looked away, feeling undeserving of his praise. If he only knew what kind of woman she really was, he wouldn't stare at her with those soft hazel eyes all aglow.

Gently he took her elbow. "Michael asked me to find you. He wants to get back to Larkin's Glen."

Her head shot up in alarm. "Is he all right?"

"Just hungry. All the women's talk of good food got to his stomach," Stewart said with a grin. He winked, sending shock waves through Charlotte's heart.

I mustn't get involved with him, she thought with firm resolve. *There's no hope for us. Nothing can ever come of a relationship with this man.* Yet her heart refused to listen to her silent reasoning.

❧

Instead of going on their usual picnic, Charlotte and Stewart went with Michael to Larkin's Glen and partook of lunch there. Michael was obviously tired, and after a delicious meal of roast turkey, baby green peas drenched in butter, and a cranberry mold, he excused himself to lie down.

Stewart studied Charlotte as she took her last bite of lemon meringue pie. He was happy to see that her appetite had improved somewhat in the weeks since she'd arrived. She met his gaze, and a light flush colored her cheeks before she looked down at her plate, which was now empty.

"Would you care to go sit in the garden?" he asked, knowing it was her favorite spot, with the waterfall by the stream a close second.

"Yes, I'd like that," she said with a smile.

He helped her from her chair, then walked with her into the

garden. The apple and cherry trees had lost their pink and white blossoms, and growing fruit could be seen beneath their green foliage. Instead of sitting on the bench, they strolled along the flagstone path through the vast enclosed area.

"I've been wanting to speak with you," Stewart said as he gently pulled Charlotte's arm through his. She stiffened, but he ignored her reaction and kept talking. "I'm going to Manhattan tomorrow on a combination business and shopping excursion, and I'd like you to come with me."

"Oh." She stopped walking and turned toward him, her eyes wide in surprise.

"I've talked to Michael, and he agrees that it's time to see to your wardrobe."

Hastily she turned her head, exhibiting unusual interest in a patch of bright pink petunias. "I don't need anything."

Stewart inhaled swiftly, finally letting out his breath in a loud burst of air. So, they were going to go through that again. It was time to try another tack.

"Myra, listen to me. Your dress is charming, but it's beginning to show wear. Michael isn't a proud man, but he is wealthy, and for you to wear the same dress weeks on end— what do you think that tells people about Michael? That he doesn't care for his own when he has the funds to do so?"

Charlotte furrowed her brow. She smoothed the skirt with one hand, casting a glance downward. Though the material was sturdy, having gone through many washings, the hem was beginning to fray. Reluctantly she nodded.

"All right. I'll go with you."

"Excellent!" Stewart enthused, his eyes bright with anticipation. "I need to leave you now. I have several things to take care of before our excursion." He tipped his bowler while taking a few steps backward, toward the gate. "I'll pick you up at seven, and we'll leave on the morning train. Good-bye."

❧

Charlotte watched as he turned, unlatched the gate, and hurried away. She couldn't help but think his quick escape had been executed before she could change her mind.

Shaking her head, she walked to the bench and sank onto it. She bent over and fingered the graceful lily of the valley that grew nearby, taking pleasure in the sweet fragrance of the tiny white, bell-shaped flowers.

But her thoughts soon turned to the lie she lived, and a chill coursed up her spine. Each day the sharp teeth of deceit ate away at her, until she felt that soon there would be nothing left. And was Michael really any better for her silence? Except for a temporary lull when he was in high spirits, his health seemed no better. And often she'd seen that despondent look in his eyes when he thought no one was watching.

Letting out a sigh, Charlotte left the beauty of the garden and soon found herself in the front parlor, again staring somberly at the painting. Why Anna's painting drew her in she couldn't say, but it did. And why it produced such sorrow and longing in her was a mystery Charlotte wished she could unravel.

Beth hustled in and stopped short, dropping her reticule when she saw Charlotte. "Oh! Pardon me, Miss. I thought this room was empty. I was looking for the key to my mother's house. She's away, and I need to go and water her plants. The key must have fallen out of my bag earlier." She moved to leave.

"I haven't seen it," Charlotte said quickly, glad for the maid's presence to dispel her gloomy thoughts. "Go ahead and look. I'll help you."

The key was soon found, the vase of flowers that Beth had knocked over was righted, and the spill cleaned. The maid then left for her day off, and Charlotte was alone again. A strange tenseness built inside her with each passing hour. She was disappointed when Michael didn't come down for dinner. Left to her tormenting thoughts, Charlotte snapped at the help in her frustration and ate little of what Tildy prepared. Why did she feel like a kettle that was dangerously close to boiling over?

Edgy, she strolled through the garden, hoping the night air would give welcome relief. The breeze cooled her face, yet did nothing for her mind. The moon was almost full, and she stopped and stared up at it, her hands clenched at her sides.

Had God really used her to help that little girl? Why had Amanda been so drawn to her. . .unless perhaps it was the other way around—that God had used Amanda to help her. The child's vulnerability and trust had touched something deep within Charlotte, more so when she'd heard Amanda's story.

"Why, God?" Charlotte snapped at the dark sky. "Why now? If You really do care, why did I have to live the childhood I did—with no father, with a prostitute for a mother? With a man, who I thought was my husband, who beat me?" A tear rolled past her lower lashes and slipped down her cheek.

"I'm nothing," she whispered. "I'm dirt. Eric said so many times. He was right."

All anger drained from her as suddenly as it had come, and she sank to the damp grass, heedless of ruining her skirt. Her hand reached out to a nearby flower bed. Numb, she scooped up the soil, letting it trickle through her fingers.

"I'm stained, tarnished, defiled. . . . I can never be new, never start over again," she whispered in resignation as she dully watched the brown grains fall to the grass.

Come unto me. . . .

The gentle words whispered to her heart, filling Charlotte with incredible longing. She slowly shook her head. "I've done too many wicked things."

. . .all ye that labour and are heavy laden. . .

Pain burned through the bridge of her nose, and sudden hot tears filled her eyes. "I'm no good."

. . .and I will give you rest. . . .

"It's too late for me to start over," she softly insisted, another tear rolling down her cheek. She swiped it away with a dirty fist.

. . .Take my yoke upon you, and learn of me. . .

"I wish I could, but I can't." Emotion choked her words.

. . .for I am meek and lowly in heart. . . .

Charlotte closed her eyes, and more tears fell.

. . .and ye shall find rest unto your souls. For my yoke is easy, and my burden is light.

She collapsed to the ground and buried her face against her sleeve. Her hand clutched blades of grass and uprooted them. Dry sobs convulsed her.

Come to me, Daughter. . . . Return to me. . . .

The soothing words spoke deep to her heart, cajoling, building up a deep yearning within her. . .a promise of water to parched ground. And she was unwilling to fight any longer.

"Yes," she whispered. "I don't understand why You would want me or love me, but I'm Yours, Lord. I'm Yours. . . ."

Incredible warmth filled her. Charlotte felt such heaviness lift from her shoulders that she thought she might float away. She straightened and blinked up at the sky and the garden surrounding her. Everything appeared to be the same, but she sensed a difference within and smiled through her tears.

She truly belonged to God. For some reason she probably would never understand, He loved her. Really loved her.

On the heels of that knowledge came another thought: She could no longer live in the web of deceit she'd spun. It hadn't brought her the peace she sought. Tomorrow, she would tell Stewart the truth—no matter the consequences to her.

nine

Charlotte rose before dawn, washed, and dressed. She ate a hurried meal in the kitchen, the rotund cook clucking at her haste, and then visited the garden one last time. Though she felt as if she were taking a step in the right direction, her decision to leave wasn't any easier to bear.

Mrs. Manning found her sitting on the bench, staring soulfully into space. Her narrowed eyes scanned Charlotte from head to foot, and the housekeeper frowned. "What happened to your dress? There's grass stains all over the skirt. I suppose it's a good thing you're going to Manhattan to get a new wardrobe all right, though I think Mr. Larkin should send a chaperone along, as well. But I ain't one to interfere. Still, it's a crying shame you have to be seen in such a condition. Good thing he don't know. He wouldn't approve, not at all."

"Is that for me?" Charlotte responded with a weary sigh, not feeling up to another of the housekeeper's ramblings. She nodded toward the envelope the woman carried.

Mrs. Manning's frown deepened as she handed Charlotte the envelope. "Your uncle wanted you to have this. He's not feeling well enough to come down and see you off. He said it was to be used only for fun. Said he wanted you to have a memorable time while you was there."

Charlotte furrowed her brow. "He's not worse?"

Mrs. Manning shrugged. "About the same. I've already called the doctor."

"The doctor?" Charlotte repeated softly. "Perhaps I shouldn't go. . . ."

The older woman shook her head. "That would only serve to make Mr. Larkin feel guilty—especially if he knew he was the cause of your staying. Doctor's visits aren't unusual at Larkin's Glen."

"Yes, I suppose you're right." Charlotte looked down at the envelope she held. She waited an interminable time for the housekeeper to leave, and at last she did so.

Charlotte opened the flap and withdrew a large number of bills. Because she was accustomed to English pounds, she had no idea how much she held. But she knew it must be a lot. Tears filled her eyes at Michael's generosity.

Of course she couldn't accept it. She had no right.

Carefully she slipped the paper money back into the envelope and returned to her room, heavy of heart. She'd made up her mind not to return to Larkin's Glen. This excursion gave her the opportunity she needed to make a clean break.

Sitting at the small oak desk near the window, she pulled out the blotter and dipped a pen into the inkwell, then poised it above a sheet of blank paper.

What on earth could she say? How could she tell Michael of her treachery? How could she cause him such pain?

Biting her lower lip, Charlotte wrote a few words, but upon looking at them, they seemed heartless, cold. She crumpled the paper and threw it in the waste bin. She couldn't do it. Stewart would have to tell Michael later—after she'd gone.

Crossing her arms over the desk, Charlotte lowered her head, the pain running too deep for tears. Had she known what the future held the day she walked off the *Carpathia,* she never would have taken the name of Myra Flannigan. Her heart had grown fond of Larkin's Glen, of Michael, of the small country church and the people there. And she knew with a sense of despair that what she felt for Stewart exceeded mere fondness.

A noisy motorcar in the distance broke the silence, and a bittersweet smile tugged at Charlotte's lips. How she would miss everything about that man! From the way his hazel eyes glowed with childish exuberance when he played his fiddle, to that noisy, smelly motorcar that was his pride and joy.

The tears came then, and hastily she wiped them away, jumped up from the chair, and laid the envelope of money on the dresser where someone would be sure to see it. She turned to go, then hesitated.

Suppose Michael had told Stewart of his plan to provide her with spending money. Wouldn't he think it odd if she didn't bring any with her? Of course, once she told him the truth about her deceit, it wouldn't matter. Yet she might need money to buy food until she found a position. She could always post the money to Michael later. She finally withdrew one of the bills from the envelope and stuffed it in her bodice. The weather was too warm for her to wear her coat, and she didn't have a reticule. She hoped they would find someone needy who could use her coat.

She hurried to the stairs and came to an abrupt stop halfway down. Stewart stood on the landing and looked up, brows raised in surprise.

"Mrs. Manning told me you were in the garden."

"I needed to run up to my room. . . . Perhaps I should check on Michael before we go." She really did want to see him one last time, though it would be difficult.

Stewart shook his head. "I wanted to do the same, but Mrs. Manning told me he was sleeping. Are you ready?"

She nodded and took the last few steps down.

He studied her face intently. "You look upset."

"It's just that I hate to leave—what with Michael sick and all." Charlotte turned away, unable to look into Stewart's eyes.

"He'll be all right. We'll be back tomorrow."

His words tried to reassure, but they made Charlotte feel worse. There would be no tomorrow for her at Larkin's Glen.

❧

The drive to the station seemed longer than usual, as did the train ride into Manhattan. Something urged Charlotte to tell Stewart the truth, but her well-laid plans crumbled to dust, and each time she opened her mouth to speak, she clamped it shut again. It might be wrong, but she wanted this last day with Stewart. A carefree day to remember, the final day he would look upon her as someone cherished. For she knew that once she told him the truth, he would despise her.

Manhattan was exactly as Charlotte remembered—only busier, since it was approaching midday. Streetcars and motorcars chugged and rattled past the rows upon rows of tall buildings, and honking horns lent their confusion to the cacophony. Horses and carriages of all kinds clip-clopped by, vying for space on the congested streets, which were wet from a recent rainfall. A few hardy hawkers stood on the sidewalks at the corners, shouting out their wares.

Stewart stopped to purchase a newspaper from a scrawny young paper boy and must have tipped him generously, judging by the toothy smile and the exuberant "Thanks, Mister!" the brown-eyed lad gave him in return.

Stewart turned to her and smiled. "Before I take you on your first subway ride through Manhattan, what do you say we eat an early lunch? I know the perfect place. Not grand, mind you, but the food is excellent."

"All right." Charlotte wasn't all that hungry, but she wanted to put off riding the unknown subway. Why anyone would want to go under the earth's surface was beyond her reasoning. Yet after all she'd endured in her twenty years, she felt she could withstand that, as well.

They hailed a cab. Stewart handed Charlotte up into the enclosed area, then turned to the driver. "Maretti's, please."

The driver arched one eyebrow, but nodded and shook the horses' reins. Soon Stewart and Charlotte were seated in a small, charming restaurant with round tables bearing red-and-white-checkered cloths and lit candles. A smiling violinist, with bushy black eyebrows and mustache, hovered near and played to them while Charlotte sampled the Italian cuisine.

She set down her fork and fanned her mouth with a gentle wave of her fingers.

"Hot?" Stewart asked.

Charlotte nodded and blinked. "Not spicy. Just hot. I do like the tomato and cheese, though. What is this called again?"

"Lasagna."

Stewart's smiling eyes met hers across the table. When the violinist moved away, Stewart reached past the flickering candle and covered her hand, which rested near her plate.

"It's a pleasure seeing everything through your eyes, Myra. I feel as if I'm experiencing the city for the first time."

Charlotte's eyes flicked down to the table, heat rushing through her at his warm, gentle touch. He gave her fingers a squeeze before removing his hand.

"Would you like some spumoni?" he asked later, when a waiter removed their empty plates.

"I. . .suppose," she said hesitantly, her brow furrowing.

He laughed. "I assure you, you won't be disappointed."

And she wasn't. The layered, soft ice cream dessert thickly speckled with candied fruit and pistachio nuts was a treat to her taste buds.

After they'd eaten, Stewart took her arm and walked beside her along the street to a stairway leading downward. The subway.

Charlotte gripped the black rails at the side as she took the stone stairs. It seemed important to Stewart that she experience this, and she didn't want to disappoint him.

They entered a cavernous room, surprisingly well lit. At the edge of the station's platform lay a rail and long tunnel— also lit—that led to who only knew where on both sides. Their footsteps echoed on the concrete floor as they headed for a small ticket booth. An elderly man with mutton chop whiskers stood on the other side of the bronze grille window, selling tickets. Four men waited in line in front of them, and Stewart turned to Charlotte.

"If you'd like to sit down while I purchase our tickets, there are several benches along the wall."

Gratefully Charlotte agreed, and she made her way to one of the secluded benches. She wasn't accustomed to so much walking. They must have covered at least a fourth of the large, busy city! Soon Stewart joined her, sitting next to her on the wooden seat. They were alone in their corner by the wall.

His eyes sparkled as he put one arm behind her along the top of the bench. "So what do you think of your first real taste of Manhattan so far?"

"It's certainly busy. Much like London."

Stewart's smile faded, and his brows drew downward. "Are you homesick, Myra?"

"No. Why do you ask?"

"I don't know. You seem. . .withdrawn. I'm glad you're not pining for England, though. I've come to really enjoy your company."

His expression grew serious, increasing her pulse rate by half. His hand slowly lifted, and his fingers stroked her cheek. She was mesmerized by the look in his eyes.

"And I want you to know. . ."

Whatever else he was about to say was cut off by a loud racket, steadily increasing in volume until it became a roar in Charlotte's ears. The bench vibrated beneath her, and Charlotte clutched his arm, her eyes growing wide.

"Relax." He moved his hand to cover hers. "It's only the train. Sound amplifies underground."

A terrible screeching of brakes heralded the train as it came into sight and slowed to a stop in front of the platform. Several passengers disembarked, including a small child with his father, all with calm expressions on their faces. Charlotte relaxed.

Once they were inside and the train was on its way, Charlotte looked out at the stone walls they sped past, a bit disappointed. Subways certainly weren't intended for the view.

"I thought we would go to the Ladies Mile to acquire your wardrobe," Stewart said. "It has some of the largest and finest stores in the city. Macy's, for instance."

"Oh, no." Charlotte turned his way. "I don't want anything expensive. Just something small and simple."

Stewart's brows drew down and he opened his mouth to protest.

"Please, Stewart."

He exhaled a short breath. "All right, Myra. Though Michael won't be too happy about it. He told me to get you the finest."

"Something simple is all I want."

Stewart pursed his lips, nodded, and unfolded his newspaper, and she turned to look back out the window.

ॐ

Charlotte frowned as Stewart opened the carved door with the gold engraved nameplate underneath a rose canvas awning. She noted the boutique's posh pink, ivory, and gold interior.

"This is not simple," she accused in a soft voice.

Stewart avoided her gaze. "Sure it is. It's small—just what you asked for."

"Stewart. . ."

"Good afternoon, Sir, Madam." A bespectacled woman in a navy blue silk dress hurried toward them. "My name is Madam Rosalie. Is there some way I may be of service to you today?"

"No, thank you."

"Yes, please."

Charlotte and Stewart spoke at the same time, eliciting a raised brow from the tiny, dark-headed woman facing them. Charlotte felt heat overwhelm her cheeks.

"The lady needs a complete wardrobe. Money is no object," Stewart inserted smoothly before Charlotte could open her mouth again.

The woman intently eyed Charlotte's curvaceous form. Her brow again lifted when she noticed the grass stains on the gray linen. "Of course," she murmured, her brown eyes curious as they lifted to Charlotte. "It will be a pleasure to outfit a woman with such a fine figure."

"Excellent. Then I leave her in your capable hands, Madam Rosalie. I've business to attend to." Stewart tipped his hat to Charlotte, one side of his mouth turning upward in a boyish grin when he caught her blazing eyes. "I shall return in two hours."

"I look forward to it," Charlotte said, unsmiling.

His eyes twinkled at her, and she felt as if she could cheerfully hit him.

Throughout the numerous fittings of chiffons, organdies, silks, and fine linens, Charlotte fumed at how Stewart had manipulated her into this predicament. She felt terrible spending Michael's money when she had no right, and when her eye caught sight of the price tags, discreetly hidden from view inside the sleeves of the exquisite dresses, she softly groaned. Macy's likely would have been less expensive than this! She only hoped Stewart would be able to get a refund for the unworn dresses. Madame Rosalie told her that once alterations were made, the clothes would be ready in two days. Stewart would know the truth tomorrow and could cancel the order.

Madam Rosalie was all charm, oohing and ahhing over each outfit Charlotte tried on. When she showed her a line of shimmering, lace-edged evening gowns, Charlotte firmly refused. Her pleas that Madam Rosalie had selected too much fell on deaf ears—the woman assured Charlotte that her husband had given her full authority to outfit Charlotte with an entire summer wardrobe.

Charlotte hastily looked away, deciding it would be better not to correct the woman's false assumptions concerning her and Stewart. It would sound irregular if she were to say anything to the contrary, so she kept silent and went along with the proceedings.

After the dresses came gloves, stockings, garters, corsets, and hats—all of which Madam Rosalie had in abundant supply. At last the ordeal was over, and Charlotte was outfitted in a cinnamon-colored day dress of fine linen needing no alterations, and the gray dress she'd worn for weeks was summarily disposed of. According to the gilt enamel clock sitting on a nearby marble table, Charlotte still had almost thirty minutes before Stewart returned.

"Would you care for some tea or coffee while you wait?" Madam asked solicitously, as Charlotte headed for the settee.

"No, thank you."

A sudden loud crash sounded outside, followed by a horse's neighing and a stream of heated words in a foreign language.

Charlotte hurried to the door and opened it, Madam Rosalie behind her. A horse cart full of colorful flowers had lost a wheel on the street directly in front of the shop. A short man jumped down from the driver's seat and pulled at his thick, graying hair when he saw the damage. His heated words became a wail as he shook his head in despair; he turned and shook a brown fist at the horse, then at his cart. Traffic streamed by him, drivers curious as they surveyed the scene. But no one stopped to help.

Without thinking about what she was doing, Charlotte hurried down the steps to the distraught man.

He pivoted her way. "The flowersah. I must get them to the church for the wedding. If I am late—no business." He threw his hands up in the air. "If no business, my family—they do not eat!"

Charlotte floundered for something to say that could help. "Perhaps you can get another cart from somewhere nearby?"

His dark brow remained puckered in a frown. "I cannot leave my flowersah. Someone may take them."

Charlotte looked at the white, pink, and peach blossoms. "I could watch them for you until you return."

His thick black brows sailed upward. "You would do that for Ricardo? Oh, grazie, grazie, Signorina! My brother's shop—it is not far. I will borrow his cart." He offered her a beaming smile and plucked a creamy rose from its resting place amid the other blossoms.

"For you." He offered the perfectly shaped flower, just beginning to open its velvety petals. "For your kindness."

"Thank you." Charlotte took the flower, her gaze lingering on the graceful petals long after the little man had hurried away. She lifted it to her nose, inhaling its sweet perfume.

Her gaze lifted to the stairs, where Madam Rosalie stood with one eyebrow raised. Obviously the woman was not in favor of Charlotte's behavior.

Charlotte lifted her chin, staring back.

Madam Rosalie drew herself up and marched into her shop. However, Charlotte noticed that she frequently peeked out the louvered window. She assumed the woman paid such close attention to her because Charlotte wore merchandise not yet paid for.

Idly she watched the passing traffic, her mind trying to formulate the words she must soon tell Stewart. She would reveal her true identity, but she wouldn't go deeply into the reasons why she'd started the charade—just that she had. She prayed Michael wouldn't take the news too badly and felt like a coward for not facing him. She'd grown close to the kind Irishman, even beginning to think of him as her true uncle. She couldn't bear to see the pain her lie would cost him.

Tears threatened, and she again lowered her face, raising the fragrant blossom to her nose. If Stewart didn't take her to jail, perhaps she could obtain employment at one of the many department stores in the area. Or maybe she should seek domestic service as a maid, like Beth. She could certainly do as well if not better than the clumsy maid. . . .

"Well, well, well. If it isn't my dear Charlotte."

The blossom dropped from Charlotte's suddenly nerveless fingers. Her eyes widened, and her mouth went dry. Unbelieving, she spun around, her heart hammering in her ears.

Eric!

ten

"Bonjour." He tipped his hat to her, his dark blue eyes gleaming evilly in his handsome face. Every strand of his blond hair lay fashionably in position, and from the looks of his fine clothes, he hadn't suffered any.

"Eric. . .you—you didn't die," Charlotte whispered, a trembling hand going to her bodice. She felt as if her heart might leap out of her chest. "But your name wasn't on the survivors' list!"

Eric studied her with unruffled calm. "Nor was yours, and yet I see you also deed not perish."

"But—how. . ."

"I went to your stateroom and took a nightdress. On ze *Carpathia,* I removed ze dress and wrapper, as well as ze hat I borrowed."

Charlotte felt sick to her stomach. "You pretended to be a woman to save your life?"

His eyes narrowed. "I deed what I must to survive."

She shook her head, still confused. "But your name. . ."

His mouth drew into a thin line. Clearly he was growing agitated, and Charlotte took a few steps backward.

"I took ze name of one of ze men I played cards wiz in ze smoke room," he explained. "Philip Rawlins. I knew he had no family."

"But—but how did you know he was dead?"

His lips turned upward in a cold smile, and Charlotte felt faint. "You killed him, didn't you," she said in a shaky whisper.

"Let's just say I knew."

Charlotte's eyes briefly fluttered shut, and she put a hand to the side of the cart for support. Eric took a few steps, closing the distance between them.

116

"Where are zey?" he said, his expression hardening.

Charlotte swallowed hard. "What are you talking about?"

"You know exactly what I'm talking about." He grabbed her upper arms and squeezed. A tic jumped in his cheek, and his eyes turned to blue fire. "I know of your leetle visit to my stateroom before ze *Titanic* went down. I want ze diamonds and ze deed, Charlotte." He tightened his hold, making her wince. "Now!"

"I don't have them," she cried softly. When the pressure increased even more, she blurted, "I did, but they're gone."

Eric glared at her with narrowed eyes. "Where are zey?"

"I don't know." She forced herself to return his stare, to fight down the rising panic. "I don't have them anymore."

He continued to search her eyes, as if to see if she were telling the truth. "You always were a little fool," he rasped. Exhaling sharply, he gave her a little shake, then abruptly let go. She crossed her arms, putting her hands to the sleeves where his fingers had bit in, and rubbed the bruised flesh tenderly.

He followed her gesture with his eyes and smiled. She shivered.

His gaze lowered to her bodice, the smile fading as he lifted his hand and plucked something from the edge of her neckline. The bill that was in the envelope of money Michael had given her! A corner must have worked its way up her corset with all the previous fittings. Inwardly she groaned when she saw the greed light his eyes. He looked with interest at her expensive new gown, then back at the bill in his hand.

"It seems fate has brought us together again, Charlotte." He pocketed the money. "In fact, I think it beneficial zat we renew our acquaintance. My hotel is not far from here. Come."

The old fear threatened to swamp her when he took hold of her upper arm and started to walk off, but she stood her ground, refusing to budge.

"No," she vehemently whispered. "I don't belong to you

anymore. I never did, as you so explicitly told me before you left my stateroom that night."

His eyebrow raised, and he regarded her askance, his expression almost bored. "Au contraire, my pet. You do belong to me—marriage or no. I own you. You are mine."

"No, Eric. I'm different now. Things have changed. I've changed. I can never go back to that kind of life."

"Different?" He sneered down at her. "You are dirt, Charlotte. A harlot like your mother. You cannot change."

The words speared her, but she shook her head. "I found Someone who loves me. I belong to Him now."

"Loves you?" he said, his voice mocking. "And does zis lover of yours know of your former life wiz me? Or perhaps he vows his love to have his way weeth you? Hmmm?"

"No, Eric. I'm not talking about the love of a man. I'm talking about the love of God."

His face became mottled with rage, and he grabbed both her arms and shook her hard. "Don't you dare speak to me of God," he rasped, his voice trembling with barely suppressed anger. "I don't even want to hear His name! Do you understand?"

Charlotte's eyes widened, and she nodded.

He fought for control, obviously realizing he was drawing curious stares from passersby. "You are mine, Charlotte," he said more smoothly. "I paid a great deal of money for you, and I will not let you go so easily."

"Please, Eric," she tried again, beginning to panic. "You've obviously done well for yourself. Please let me go and pretend you never saw me."

He smiled. "Oh, but I don't want to pretend I never saw you. Your exceptional talents assure me of making more zen I could alone."

He withdrew Michael's bill from his pocket and held it up between thumb and forefinger. "Perhaps we should begin by fleecing whoever gave you this? Hmmm?" His eyes narrowed in speculation. "Just where have you been zese past months, Charlotte? Who gave you zis and bought you zat expensive gown?"

Never! Never would she tell him about Michael or Stewart.

Stewart! He would be back any minute. She had to get Eric out of here and fast.

"I need a few days to tie things up. I can't just disappear into thin air." Her eyes flicked nervously beyond him, and her heart plummeted. Stewart was walking across the street half a block away.

"You have to go now," she said hurriedly, searching her mind for words to get him to leave. "If I'm seen with you, it could mean trouble for both of us. Trust me. I know what I'm talking about."

Eric frowned, as though undecided. "Tonight, Charlotte. You will meet me tonight at ze subway station on Twenty-eighth Street at nine o'clock. . .or I will come looking for you."

She shivered at his ominous words, but didn't reply. She had no intention of seeking Eric—tonight or any night. As though he read her mind, his mouth turned up in a wicked grin.

"I have ways of finding things out, Charlotte, as you well know. It would be a simple matter for me to discover where you've been hiding and whom you've been hiding wiz. If you cross me, you will live to regret it. As will your friends."

His low words fell like sharp stones around her, cutting into her heart and her spirit.

❧

Stewart dodged a streetcar, impatient as he waited for it to rumble past. Who was that man with Myra? When he'd caught sight of them across the street, he noticed they were in deep conversation. And why was she standing outside the shop next to a broken flower cart?

When Stewart was about ten feet from them, the man turned and walked past Stewart without looking his way. Stewart looked after him curiously, then his gaze cut to Myra. She trembled like a leaf in a summer storm, her face as white as the crushed blossom on the ground in front of her.

"Myra?" Stewart hurried to her, gently taking her shoulders in concern. "Who was that man? What did he say to you?" he asked loudly.

She stared beyond him, her eyes going wide. Stewart turned to look.

The man had stopped walking and was now watching them, his expression one of supreme interest. A smile crooked his mouth as he tipped his hat, inclining his head their way. Then he turned and continued down the street.

Stewart felt a tremor run through her. "Myra. . .?"

"I'm not feeling well," she whispered. He watched as a shutter seemed to fall over her eyes, as it had so many times in the past, blocking him out. "I'd like to go to the hotel now and lie down."

"Did he say something indecent? Is that why you're so shaken?" He frowned and studied the retreating figure. "Perhaps I should go talk to him."

Her hand shot to his arm. "Please, Stewart, just let it be. It–it was nothing. I think the lasagna didn't agree with me, and–and the fittings were so long."

He looked into her upturned face. Her eyes were frantic.

"Myra. . ."

She attempted a smile, which fell short. "I'm certain I'll feel better soon."

He hesitated, then nodded. "After I settle the bill with Madam Rosalie, we'll find a nearby hotel." He took her arm, but she shook her head.

"I–I promised I'd watch the cart."

"The cart?" Stewart looked in confusion at the broken flower cart, then at her. "You promised whom?"

"A nice old man. He–he went to get his brother's wagon."

Stewart shook his head, puzzled. "All right. Then I'll stay with you." He wasn't about to leave her alone again.

They waited, not speaking, until, a few minutes later, a horse-driven wagon pulled up behind the flower cart. The man in the driver's seat beamed a smile their way, lifting his hat a few inches off his head.

"Grazie, Signorina. I owe you many thanks."

She didn't answer, but only gave him a wan smile in return.

Inside Madam Rosalie's, Stewart paid for the dress Myra wore and was told he could make the remainder of the payment when the rest of the gowns were ready.

"I'll settle the entire bill now, and I also want to pay to have them delivered to Ithaca," he insisted.

Myra put a hand to his arm. "I really think you should wait."

"We're leaving tomorrow," he reminded her patiently, "and the gowns won't be finished by then." He signed the voucher, confused by the sudden bleak look in Myra's eyes.

Once they arrived at the hotel, she gave him a faded smile before closing the door to her room. Stewart ran a hand along the back of his neck as he walked to his own room.

Something was very wrong. And before they left for Penn Station in the morning, Stewart determined to find out what.

⁂

Charlotte stared at the carved walls and shuddered. She knew Stewart would soon come to escort her to dinner, but she didn't see how she could eat. Since he left her at her room's door two hours earlier, she'd done nothing but stare into space, unable to believe the appalling circumstances in which she now found herself. She replayed them over and over in her mind.

Eric was alive!

Her eyes slid shut, and she felt dizzy. How could this happen? And why now? Why now, when she'd so recently given her life to God?

She stood and began to pace the deep-pile carpet. Knowing the evil of which Eric was capable, Charlotte realized she had no choice but to meet him tonight. Now that he'd seen her with Stewart, Charlotte was certain Eric could easily discover anything about her he wanted to know. And she knew his threats weren't idle. If he were crossed, he would seek revenge from whomever he felt was responsible.

And that included Michael and Stewart.

Charlotte wrung her hands. "Why, God? Why now?"

Silence met her pleas.

She turned to the mirror on the wall and stared at the ghost that looked back at her. With jerky movements, she anchored several pins back into place that had come loose from her upswept hair.

Perhaps she could try again to persuade Eric to leave her alone, tell him that she wouldn't be of any use to him, that she really had changed. . . .

She uttered a dry, humorless laugh. Persuade Eric to do something contrary to his iron will? Never.

A knock sounded, and Charlotte started; then she turned to stare at the door. She would need to draw on every bit of her acting ability to convince Stewart that nothing was wrong so he wouldn't suspect anything. Forcing her mind to go blank, she concentrated on letting her tense facial muscles relax, even managing a small welcoming smile as she headed toward the door.

❧

"Next time we come to Manhattan, I'll take you to Madison Square Garden," Stewart said. "It boasts the largest restaurant in New York City. And the Metropolitan Life Tower is the tallest building—it rises fifty stories."

"Really?" Myra beamed him a wide smile.

He studied her too bright eyes and frowned. "Yes. . . . And perhaps we'll take a carriage ride around Central Park or visit Times Square."

"It sounds simply fascinating," she said.

Stewart thought that she seemed overly nervous tonight—laughing strangely and at the oddest moments.

The waiter came with dessert, and Myra shook her head. "Oh, no, please. I couldn't eat another bite."

Stewart glanced at her plate of barely touched food, but chose not to comment. "In that case, what do you say we take that ride around Central Park now?"

The stiff smile left her face, and she opened her mouth, as if to refuse, then her features softened. "Yes, I think I would like that very much."

He took her arm, and they left the plush hotel restaurant. Stewart hailed an open carriage, then took her gloved hand to assist her up into the seat. She tensed, her eyes darting around the area, before she offered him a faint smile and stepped up into the carriage.

Stewart took his place beside her, and the driver turned toward him, a big smile on his craggy face. "Where to, Sir?"

"Once around Central Park."

The driver tipped his hat. "Very good, Sir."

Charlotte relaxed against Stewart, listening to the hollow clip-clop of horses' hooves and trying to drown out the worry that Eric might be close by. . .watching.

When Stewart took her hand, she didn't pull away but held tightly. Perhaps this carriage ride was a foolish mistake, but Charlotte wanted to stretch the day, wanted to hold on to every moment before she must part with him for good. She didn't want to think about telling him of her charade. So much had changed since this morning when they'd left Larkin's Glen. Now she knew that to protect the lives of those she'd grown to love, she couldn't tell Stewart about Eric, as she'd planned to. Which meant she could tell him nothing of her past.

She leaned her head back against the seat, determined to forget what lay ahead and enjoy this last hour with the man she loved. The dusky purple of twilight deepened, and hazy stars dotted the darkening sky. The tree-filled park, with its impeccably groomed shrubs, was a verdant oasis in the midst of the towering buildings. A tranquil pond with swans floating on its dark, glassy surface came into view as the carriage moved onto one of the meandering paths bordered with colorful flowers. Charlotte relaxed, determined to forget the immediate future.

Almost without realizing she'd done so, she leaned her head against Stewart's shoulder. The slow clop-clopping of horses' hooves, the trilling bird song in the trees, and the far-away lilt of laughter were the only sounds to be heard in the cooling evening air.

The carriage had gone halfway around the park when Stewart broke the silence between them and squeezed her hand. "I'm glad you came with me to Manhattan. I've wanted to speak to you before now, but it never seemed like the right opportunity. You see, I've come to care a great deal for you, Myra."

His low words shattered her calm as swiftly as hail destroys a crop. She straightened and faced him. His eyes glowed, and he lifted a hand to brush her cheek with the back of his fingers.

"No," she whispered, eyes widening in apprehension. "Don't say it."

"I have to say it," he insisted softly. "Since you've come into my life I can think of little else but you. My profession used to be the most important aspect of my existence—I never entertained the thought of love, much less marriage. Not until a few months ago, when you came to Larkin's Glen, that is."

His words sent a shaft of bittersweet pain slicing through her, and she laid trembling fingers over his mouth. "Please, Stewart. Don't do this."

"I love you, Myra," he said, his warm breath fanning over her fingers and sending tiny little shivers through her.

"You can't love me," she argued, a catch in her voice as he pulled her hand away and lowered his head toward her.

"It's too late for that."

When his lips touched hers, she didn't resist. Soon he would be out of her life for good, and that knowledge spurred her to wrap her arms around his neck and return his kiss with fervor. He stiffened momentarily, then drew her closer. After a moment he lifted his head, his eyes anguished.

"You're crying!" he exclaimed softly. "Why are you crying?"

She shook her head, wiping the tears away with an unsteady hand.

"Myra. . .?"

"I think we should go back to the hotel now," she said, trying to speak in an even voice, but failing miserably.

Stewart wiped a tear from her chin with the tip of his index finger, his eyes questioning, pained, but he only nodded. Leaning forward, he tapped the driver on the shoulder.

"Take us back to the Waldorf Astoria."

During the ride back, Stewart held her hand, gently stroking her fingers with his thumb. The gesture was sweet torture to Charlotte, but she didn't pull away.

She tried to maintain control once they entered the hotel and took the lift to their floor, but with each step closer to her room, she realized their time together was almost at an end.

At her door, Stewart attempted a smile, though concern still lingered in his eyes. "I'll come for you at six in the morning. Our train leaves at seven fifteen, but I want to eat before we board—at least feed you more than an orange this time." His wan attempt at humor fell flat.

She studied his strong features, his soft hazel eyes, his firm, sensitive mouth, knowing it was the last time she'd ever do so. He'd shown her gentleness, consideration, and he had helped her find her way to God. And he'd taught her the true meaning of love. She would miss him dearly.

Without thought, she cupped his face with one hand. "Good-bye, Stewart."

His brow furrowed into a puzzled frown. "You mean good night, of course."

"Of course. Good night." She dropped her hand away from his jaw and entered her room. Before closing the door, she looked once more into his troubled eyes. "And thank you."

"For what?" he asked, his dark, brows slanting downward.

"For being you. For making my life a little brighter."

She closed the door with a soft click.

❧

Stewart paced the length of his hotel suite, running a hand along the back of his neck. He walked to the window, again looking below at the buildings on the other side of the street—now closed—and at the several carriages parked along the road next to the hotel.

He spun away from the window and began to pace again.

Myra's odd parting words filtered through his mind as they had done repeatedly since he'd left her at her door almost an hour ago. Why did he feel so uneasy? Why had she reacted so strangely in the carriage when he'd kissed her? And what on earth had made her cry?

He came to an abrupt halt and stared at the gold curlicues in the wallpaper. "What if there's someone she cares for? Someone she left behind in London?"

Shaking his head, he dismissed that idea and began to pace again. If she loved another, would she have responded so strongly to his kiss—both tonight and previously? Each time he'd taken her in his arms, Stewart had felt her love, felt as if she were expressing to him what she couldn't say in words.

Yet, why couldn't she vocalize her feelings for him? She wasn't shy—quiet, yes, but not shy. And very secretive.

"All right," he told the gas table lamp. "Let's see where we stand. Fact number one: Myra is running from something—or someone—and it is greatly troubling her. Assumption: Someone abused her in the past, making it difficult for her to enter into any kind of relationship." He ticked off each statement on his fingers as he spoke.

"Fact number two: Several things about Myra make no sense, and the past months have been filled with inconsistencies in her behavior. Assumption: She's not Myra at all, but someone pretending to be Myra. . . . But again that leads me to the question why. What motive could she have for this pretense? And if this theory does indeed prove to be fact and not assumption, what then happened to the real Myra?"

Stewart plowed his fingers through his hair and ran them along the back of his neck, inhaling a deep breath. He put his index finger to his thumb, the last digit left, as he exhaled forcefully. "Fact number three: She is adverse to—make that insistent against—having money spent on her. Assumption: She feels guilty for her deceit."

His pacing brought him back to the window, and he glanced out, looked away again, then did a quick double take.

A woman entered a carriage for hire that was parked in front of the hotel. Though Stewart could only see her back, the light from a nearby gas lamp had shone on her hair, causing it to glow a dull red.

He whirled, ran to the door, and wrenched it open. Quickly he covered the distance between his and Myra's rooms. He gave a sharp rap on her door, not really caring if he woke any of the other patrons.

The door hadn't been closed all the way, and it swung inward a few inches. He pushed it open the rest of the way and entered the suite. "Myra?"

A sheet of paper on the table in front of the pink velvet settee caught his attention, and a sick premonition clenched his gut.

He snatched up the hotel stationery and read the black script smeared in two places by drops of wetness.

I am grievously sorry to inform you that the true Myra Flannigan died the night of the sinking. I made her acquaintance while onboard. She was a wonderful, godly woman, a niece of whom Michael would have been proud. When I left the Carpathia *and assumed the role of Myra, I never realized what problems my pretense would cause. Nor did I realize how much I would grow to love Larkin's Glen and the people there. I can no longer bear to hurt those I've come to care about. I hope both you and Michael can one day find it in your hearts to forgive me, as I know the Lord has done. It is*

my earnest prayer that learning the truth doesn't harm
Michael. Yet I can no longer live with the lie.

Stunned, Stewart stared at the unsigned letter a moment
longer, then crumpled it in one hand and rushed out the door,
down the stairs, through the lobby, and past the shocked
doorman.

Quickly he hailed a hansom cab.

eleven

Charlotte's heart kept time with the rapid click of horses' hooves echoing on the nearly deserted road. Shopkeepers had gone home for the evening; businesses were now closed. A thick drifting cloud covered the moon, and the tall black gas lamps scattered along the street provided the only source of light.

She tightly twisted the fingers of one hand, bringing stinging pain with the action. A myriad of emotions—sorrow, fear, desperation, uncertainty—coursed through her. And she knew that, for her, time had almost run out; soon she would face Eric. That thought made the anxiety she'd experienced these past months while at Larkin's Glen seem pale in comparison.

Knowing Eric as well as she did, Charlotte was certain he wouldn't release her from his power, no matter how she pleaded. Her only way out of this predicament rested in finding a way to escape him at the earliest opportunity.

The carriage rounded a corner, and Charlotte saw the sign: Twenty-eighth Street. Her eyes fluttered shut.

Please, God, I desperately need Your help. You know how much I fear Eric. Please let no harm come to me, and help me find a way to escape him.

The carriage halted in front of the dark subway entrance. She looked toward the stairs leading downward and shivered. Her former anxiety had now become stark terror. Before she alit from the carriage, explaining to the skeptical driver that she would have to collect his money from someone inside, Charlotte again silently pleaded for God's protection.

❧

Stewart looked at the deserted streets. Dark glass, like cavernous eyes, stared at him from the faces of closed businesses

129

and warehouses. He leaned forward in the carriage. "Are you sure the woman went this way?"

"Yes, Sir. I heard her tell Henry where she wanted to go."

"Can't you go any faster?"

The driver nodded.

Stewart settled back, though his tense fingers remained curled around the top of the door. Why would she go to the subway station? She clearly hadn't enjoyed their visit there earlier. And why in the world would she go in the black of night? If she really wanted to get away, why hadn't she picked Penn Station or Grand Central and taken a train from there?

At last they arrived at Twenty-eighth Street, and Stewart had the driver pull over at the building next to the subway. He quickly paid him, telling him there was an extra five dollars in it for him if he stayed, and hurried toward the entrance. An empty carriage sat in front of the station. The driver looked disgusted.

"Did you bring a woman here?" Stewart asked. "Wearing a brown dress and having red hair?"

The driver grunted. "Said she'd collect my fee, but she's been gone five minutes at least. I've a mind to go down there."

Stewart hurriedly pulled out the same amount he'd paid his own driver and stuffed it in the man's hand. "That should cover it."

A thin scream sailed up from below. The driver's eyes widened. He slapped the reins, and the carriage took off with a loud clatter of wagon wheels and horses' hooves. Stewart spun and took the stairs down two at a time.

❧

"Please, Eric, you're hurting me," Charlotte whimpered.

"You have developed a boldness I do not appreciate," he purred, wrenching her arm higher behind her back, intensifying the pain in her shoulder. "I do not like my women to talk back."

Charlotte swallowed, afraid to say anything, tears of pain filling her eyes. They were alone in the cavernous underground room. Even the ticket master was no longer in his caged booth.

Eric smiled and released the pressure, as if realizing he'd scored a victory. "Now as I told you, you will meet Mr. Trundle tonight. You will again pretend to be my sister—we had such success wiz zat on ze *Titanic*—and you will flatter ze man wiz your charms. And I do not want to ever hear again how you are adverse to our work."

Charlotte felt sick to her stomach. She should have known better than to try to appeal to Eric one last time. There was no alternative but to seek escape whenever possible.

He looked at her dress and frowned. "It is unfortunate you must wear somezing so inappropriate, but tomorrow we will remedy zat situation. . . ."

Rapid footsteps echoed across the cement floor, and Eric's head snapped up. Surprise, then anger, flickered in his eyes.

Charlotte turned her head to look and suddenly felt faint.

"Stewart."

He looked at her briefly, his eyes unreadable, then turned his gaze Eric's way as he continued toward them. "Unhand the lady," he said, his voice low but chilling in its intensity.

Eric's eyes narrowed and he sneered. "Lady? You are seeking ze wrong woman, Sir. Zis is no lady. She belongs to me."

Stewart's eyes flickered in uncertainty, but his stony expression remained fixed. He stopped a few feet away. "I said let her go."

Instead of doing as commanded, Eric whipped her around so that her back was pressed against his chest, and snaked an arm across her throat, edging closer to the platform. Charlotte gripped his forearm, trying to pull it away as she struggled for breath.

"She is mine," Eric insisted smoothly. "I can do what I want wiz her. I bought her."

"Bought her?" Incredulity rang in Stewart's voice.

"Her mother sold her to me. In London."

Humiliated, Charlotte closed her eyes, unable to look at Stewart. The ensuing silence rang in her ears, and she wished she could sink through the floor and disappear.

"How much?"

Stewart's low words sent tremors through Charlotte. She felt Eric tense. "What?" he asked.

"How much did you pay for her?"

"One hundred pounds," Eric said, the sneer in his voice again.

Charlotte heard the sound of riffling paper and opened her eyes, curious.

Stewart withdrew a thick wad of bills from his wallet and threw them to the floor between them. They hit the cement and scattered. "That should more than cover the sum you mentioned in British pounds," he ground out through gritted teeth.

Charlotte felt as if her heart had died within her.

Eric hesitated, as though undecided, then removed his arm from her throat and thrust Charlotte away from him. She fought for balance and watched as he bent, greedily stuffing the money into his pockets. When he stood, his expression mocked her. He addressed Stewart, though his eyes remained fixed on her.

"It is your loss. She isn't worth it anymore."

Stewart inhaled sharply, and Charlotte cast an uncertain glance his way. His eyes blazed gold-green fire at Eric, and his hands clenched and unclenched at his sides.

"Now get out," Stewart growled. "And never come near her again! If you so much as come within fifty feet of her, you'll live to regret it."

Eric's eyes narrowed, but he only tipped his hat in mock salute. "A pleasure doing business with you."

Stewart took a threatening step forward, and Eric hastened to the stairs leading outside. Charlotte stood as if frozen, her gaze skittering away from Stewart. The seconds crawled by until at last the ticket agent came from somewhere and reentered his booth. He gave the two a curious glance, breaking the ominous silence with his whistled tune.

Stewart grabbed her forearm. "Come," he said abruptly, moving toward the exit. Charlotte had no choice but to go with him. Thankfully, Eric was nowhere in sight when they emerged onto the sidewalk.

The ride back to the hotel was silent, tense. Every now and then Charlotte dared to send a sidelong glance Stewart's way. He stared straight ahead, his jaw rigid, his mouth a narrow line. Not once since they'd left the subway did he look at her or address her, except for the curt order to get into the carriage.

Charlotte squirmed, uncertain and fearful of what lay ahead. When they pulled up in front of the hotel, Stewart again grabbed her above the elbow once they'd exited the buggy, his hold firm, and escorted her to the lift. When they came to the door of her room, he opened it and walked into her suite with her, then closed the door.

She turned, apprehensive, and stared at him. Doubts filtered through her mind. From what she knew of this man, she had nothing to fear. . .yet he'd given Eric money. Did he expect something in return?

"Stop looking at me that way," Stewart said gruffly. "You should know by now I'd never hurt you."

Her brow furrowed, her eyes anxious. "You bought me from Eric. How should I know what to expect from you?"

"I bought your freedom—I didn't buy you." His jaw tensed, and he motioned to the settee. "Sit. We have much to discuss."

She looked at him, uncertain.

He raised a brow. "After giving your gentleman friend over three hundred dollars, I think at least you owe me an explanation. Don't you?" Stewart turned away, swiping a hand along the back of his neck. He didn't want to lose his temper. And he was alarmingly close to doing so.

"Now," he continued, once she was seated, "you can start by giving me your name. Your real one this time."

She hesitated. "For three years I've gone by Charlotte Fontaneau, and I've grown accustomed to it." Her voice was reed thin.

Standing a few feet in front of her, he tossed his hat on the matching chair. "And before that?"

"Charleigh is what my mum called me."

"Just Charleigh? No last name?"

She shook her head. "Just Charleigh."

"And what relationship do you have to that man you were with—Eric?" The name tasted sour in his mouth.

"I–I met him when I was a flower girl in London." She paused. "He bought all my flowers and paid me compliments that first day—enough to turn my head and make me think he was a gentleman. He tricked my mum, too."

Her eyes slid shut, and he waited.

"But I didn't know until a few months after the wedding ceremony that Eric Fontaneau was no gentleman," she practically whispered.

A sick chill washed over Stewart. "That man was your husband?"

"I thought he was."

Perplexed, Stewart ran a hand through his hair and began to pace. "Perhaps you'd better start from the beginning."

Her gaze drifted down to her lap, and she pulled at the fingers of one hand. "My mum worked in a tavern. That's where I spent my life from as early as I can remember. Every day I sold flowers in the streets and parks, and when I turned fourteen, I was made to serve drinks to the men who came to the tavern at night. They paid me a great deal of notice, and soon the tavern keeper said it was time I start paying my way." She shuddered.

Stewart felt a trace of sympathy but remained silent.

"My mum begged him to wait, telling him that I wasn't fully grown, that I was still a child. He went along with it— until I turned seventeen. When one of the men grabbed me one night, I smacked him on the head with my empty tray, and the tavern keeper struck me across the face. He told me to get used to it, that I was expected to do what my mum did from then on."

Stewart stopped at the window and looked out at the dark

street below. "Go on."

Charlotte bit her lip. "I was sick with a fever that next week and wasn't able to serve drinks. My first day out, I met Eric at the park. Later he came to the tavern."

She crossed her arms, rubbing them with her hands. "He was so debonair, so full of charm, so wealthy and handsome. I'd never met anyone like him. When he offered to take me away from the tavern and into a life with him, I could scarce believe it. He—he tried to bed me, but I told him I didn't want to be like my mum, that I wanted to do it proper, after I had a husband." Her cheeks flushed with fire. "He seemed upset at first, then became even more charming and agreed. I thought I'd died and entered my own fairy tale."

Stewart spun from the window and walked her way. "And?"

"And so he married me. . .or I thought he did." She lifted tear-filled eyes up to him. "He told me the night the *Titanic* sank—after he'd beaten me almost senseless—that the marriage was a sham. That he—the son of a French count—would never marry the daughter of a harlot, and I was a fool to think he had. He said I deserved what I got. He told me a drinking friend of his owed him a favor and pretended to be a justice at the ceremony," she ended miserably.

White-hot rage coursed through Stewart and his fists clenched. He wished Eric were here right now. On second thought, maybe it was better that he wasn't. Stewart felt as if he could kill the man.

"That's why you pretended to be Myra? To escape Eric?"

Charlotte gave a swift nod, and her gaze again lowered to her lap and clenched hands. "There's more."

"I'm listening."

Charlotte nervously began to twist the fingers of one hand. "I—I associated with Eric in a life of crime when I thought I was his wife. I was afraid he'd kill me if I didn't do what he said." She kept her eyes averted.

There was a lengthy pause. "What kind of crime?"

Charlotte swallowed hard. "Thievery—con games. Eric is

a card shark, a gambler, and. . .and I know he killed a man," she added softly, her eyes drifting shut.

"How do you know?" Stewart's voice was insistent.

"Because I was there." When he said nothing more, Charlotte explained. "Eric used me as bait. I sometimes pretended to be his sister and flirted with the victims."

"And did you take them to your bed as well?"

Stewart's voice had grown hard, brittle, and Charlotte's head snapped up.

"Even if I had wanted to engage in an affair, I would have never dared. Eric would have killed me. He was very jealous. That's why he beat me the night the *Titanic* sank. He'd overheard gossip concerning me. Of course he beat me other times, too. Jealousy wasn't his only motive. Strange, isn't it? He wanted me to flirt with other men and spend time with them—but if he suspected it went beyond a peck on the cheek, he beat me black and blue."

Stewart's eyes closed.

She gave a brittle laugh. "But I'm sure you think I deserved it. I mean, after all, I am guilty, and you once said yourself the guilty have no excuse. They should be punished."

"Myra, stop it," Stewart said in an agonized voice.

"But I'm not Myra!" she exclaimed. Tears filled her eyes. "I'm Charlotte, remember? The daughter of a prostitute; a thief's lackey; a fallen woman who engaged in a sinful life with a man for three years."

"You didn't know. It's not your fault."

"But that doesn't make me any less guilty, does it? Poor Stewart," she said mockingly. "Thinking you loved a woman like me. It's a good thing you discovered the truth in time. Of course, had you let me go and never come after me, you would've been spared hearing of my sordid past. I would have found a way to escape Eric."

Stewart stared at her a long time.

"You had better get some sleep," he said, his voice tight. "We have an early train to catch."

Her eyes widened. "We? But, I thought. . ."

"What did you think?" he asked tiredly.

She blinked. "That I would stay here in Manhattan." Her voice wavered. "That you would go back alone."

"No." He took off his coat and laid it over the chair. "You're coming with me to Larkin's Glen. And just so you don't get any more ideas about running away, I'm sleeping out here on the couch. I'm a very light sleeper."

She just stared.

"Good night, Charlotte. I'm rather tired now." He put his hands to his tie. When she made no move toward the bedroom door, he looked her way. "Well?"

"Why?" she asked softly. "Why are you doing this?"

He regarded her, his expression sober. "Because you are the one who is going to face Michael and tell him the truth."

≥

Stewart tried to get into a more comfortable position. Sleep eluded him, and finally he pushed himself up off the couch and picked his way to the window in the semidark. His pants and shirt would be a wrinkled mess in the morning, but that was the least of his concerns.

Though he suspected Charlotte's pretense all along, he hadn't known just how bad things really were. That her news would devastate Michael was certain. Stewart wished he could spare his friend the pain. But what should he do concerning the information she'd told him?

He thought about the woman sleeping in the room next door. Despite all she'd confessed, he couldn't stop thinking about her. She still stirred his desire to protect her—in fact, that desire only increased when she'd told him of her past with that monster.

His hand on the curtain tightened.

Had he known the crimes of which Eric was guilty, Stewart would have sought assistance from the police before he left for the subway. Was Scotland Yard looking for Eric? And what of Charlotte?

Stewart's eyes closed. Though he failed to understand it, his love for her hadn't faded one iota. Certainly he was distressed to learn the truth and to discover that she wasn't the innocent he'd thought. But it didn't seem to make a difference concerning the way he felt about her. Amazing, considering what Clara Sterns had done to his cousin Steven.

He chuckled dryly. "God, am I as crazy as Steven? I tried to warn him about Clara. Now am I falling into the same trap?"

Groaning, he laid his forehead against the cool pane and softly banged his head against its smooth surface.

twelve

Charlotte tossed and turned in bed most of the night, unable to sleep. At one point, tears streamed down to the pillow, and she softly cried out to God, asking if He still loved her. A sudden warmth filled her, bringing with it peace, and she went to sleep with a faint smile, feeling as if God held her in His arms.

The next morning, Stewart was stiffly polite when she came from her room and they left for the train station. They boarded the train and he found them a private compartment, then offered her a sandwich from the sack he carried. "It's all I can give you, I'm afraid. My funds are severely depleted."

Charlotte felt heat rush to her face. "You shouldn't have given Eric so much money," she said from between taut lips.

Stewart looked at her from the opposite bench. "I wanted to make certain he stayed away."

Charlotte laughed bitterly. "He has never kept a promise unless it benefited him. What makes you think he will stay away from me?"

"Because if he tries to make contact with you, I will have him in jail before he knows what hit him. In fact, knowing what I do now, I almost hope he does try it."

The menacing smile on Stewart's lips made Charlotte shudder. She was afraid to ask, but needed to know. "And what about me?"

He looked up from unwrapping his sandwich. "What about you?"

"What will you do with me?"

"I told you. I'm taking you to Michael."

"And after that?"

He studied her a moment longer, then brusquely spoke. "Eat your sandwich, Charlotte."

She bit into the egg salad sandwich and forced herself to chew, though she wasn't the least bit hungry. In a few hours she'd be face to face with Michael. Her stomach felt queasy, and she put aside the food.

❧

The train ride to Ithaca had seemed to go much faster than the ride to Manhattan. Soon they were chugging along the road in Stewart's Tin Lizzy. Charlotte looked dully at the gray rocks, gorges, and streams she'd thought she would never see again. What a difference twenty-four hours could make in a person's life!

When Stewart pulled up the lane leading to Larkin's Glen, Charlotte thought she would be physically ill; she almost asked him to pull over. But the determined set to his face—as though it had been cast in stone—decided her against it, and she swallowed her growing nausea, clenching her hands on her lap into two tight fists.

Beth met them at the door. "Welcome back, Miss Flannigan, Mr. Lyons. Mr. Larkin is in his study. Would you like me to tell him you're here?"

"No," Stewart said as he handed the maid his hat. "No need to announce us." Taking Charlotte by the elbow, he escorted her along the hall to Michael's study.

Michael looked up from reading the paper, the surprised expression on his face turning into one of welcome. "Ah, so you've brought me niece back to me. And did ye find a nice wardrobe of pretty frocks, Lass?" He set down his pipe and folded the paper, looking at her expectantly.

Charlotte sent Stewart a pleading look, but he ignored it.

"Actually, Michael, there's something you must know. And I'm afraid it isn't pleasant."

Michael looked from one to the other in the ensuing silence, the smile on his face fading. "Ach, oot with it, then! And, Stewart, leave your suspense in the courtroom, if you would be of a mind." He turned to Charlotte. "Well, Lass?"

"I. . ." Her voice was raspy, and she cleared her throat.

"Perhaps you'd better sit down," Michael suggested in concern. "You look as if you may swoon. You take a chair, too, Stewart."

Charlotte sank to the hard-backed chair and clasped her hands tightly around her knees. "I—I'm so very sorry," she began, feeling as if her heart might pound out of her chest, "but I've lied to you."

Michael's bushy brows drew down in a frown. "Lied to me?"

"I. . .I'm not Myra Flannigan." Once the words were out, she felt as if a weight had been lifted off her, though she wished she could erase the shocked pain in Michael's eyes.

"Who are ye then?" he asked gruffly after a moment.

She stared at the floor and told him a portion of her childhood in the seedy part of London, talked about her tumultuous years with Eric, and ended with what happened when she left the *Titanic* and assumed Myra's identity.

"I'm so very sorry to have done this to you," she said, emotion choking her words. "I know it was horrid of me, but at the time I only wanted escape and peace. I never meant you any harm—please believe me. I even thought I was doing you a favor by giving you a niece to love."

Michael looked as if he'd been hit in the stomach, and for a long time he didn't speak. "Had I been you, I might have done the same," he said at last. " 'Tis a bitter pill ye've had to swallow, Lass. A bitter pill indeed."

Charlotte briefly closed her eyes as tears filled them. Even in his disappointment he was being kind. A kindness she didn't deserve.

"What do they call you?" he asked.

"Eric called me Charlotte, since it's a French name, and he wanted me to assume the role of a French woman. It's the name I've grown accustomed to. But my mum, she called me Charleigh."

Michael stared in shock, his face going a ghastly shade of gray. "Charleigh?"

Stewart rose from his chair in alarm. "Michael, are you ill?

Do you want me to fetch the doctor?"

Michael impatiently waved him away. His eyes remained fastened to Charlotte, a look of disbelief in them followed by dawning realization.

"And your ma, Lass," he said hoarsely. "What's her name?"

"Clementine."

Michael's mouth opened partway. Tears filled his eyes and rolled down his cheeks. "Clementine," he breathed. Then he buried his face in his large hands and wept.

Bewildered, Stewart and Charlotte looked across the room at each other, then back at Michael. Great sobs racked his body.

"Perhaps I should go," Charlotte said weakly to Stewart after several minutes had passed. She was tormented by seeing Michael's raw pain, knowing she was the cause of it.

"No!" Michael's head shot up, and his eyes softened as he studied her through his tears. "I can as yet scarcely believe 'tis true, though I see it now as plain as the nose on me face. . . ." His choked words trailed away.

Charlotte said nothing, baffled by his strange behavior.

"Michael, let me go find Mrs. Manning and get her to give you a tonic," Stewart inserted. "You look positively ill."

Michael ignored him. "Oh, my dear Charleigh. Can you ever forgive me for the wrong I've committed?"

"But it is I who wronged you," Charlotte said, shaking her head. He wasn't making any sense, and she was growing concerned. "It is I who should beg your forgiveness."

"No, Charleigh," he said, shaking his head. "Had I assumed responsibility from the first and acted like a man instead of a coward, none of this ever would have happened. You would never have had to live the life you've endured."

Charlotte furrowed her brow in confusion.

"You see, Charleigh," Michael said with a deep sigh. "I am your father."

Silence followed the startling announcement. Charlotte only stared, certain her charade had cost this poor man his anity—that he so desired a family relation, he was willing to fabricate one.

Stewart jumped up from his chair. "That's it. I'm calling for the doc."

"Sit down, Lad, and listen," Michael said brusquely, closing his eyes. "I am of sound mind, I assure you."

Stewart threw Charlotte a helpless look as he again took his chair. Obviously he felt the same way: that poor Michael had gone off the deep end and was living in a fantasy world.

Michael wearily rubbed his eyes with the fingertips of one hand. "It was twenty-one years ago that I met Clemmie. I was bold and brash and thought I knew everything there was to know, as most youths do. I was engaged to a woman in America that I didn't love and had been visiting Katie in England to escape my woes. We attended a May Day celebration outside London. I saw a young lass dancing around the maypole. She had hair the color of ripened corn, eyes of the palest green, and a laugh like tinkling bells. Ah, Clemmie was a beauty, she was. . . ." He exhaled softly.

A feeling close to dread grew within Charlotte. Her mother had had light hair and green eyes.

"Her da was a bookseller, and she came from a very strict religious background. But Clemmie, she was free as the wind. . .and as tempting as a cool, sparkling brook on a warm summer afternoon." He sadly shook his head. "After that May Day, Clemmie sneaked away from home after her chores and we'd often meet near the forest on the outskirts of London. We were two young people in love, spending every moment we could together. We never meant for anything to happen. But it did."

His eyes closed briefly. "Before I left England I assured Clemmie that I would come back for her, marry her, and take her to live in America. That I had to prepare my parents first."

Again silence permeated the room. Charlotte felt as if she'd been turned to stone. But stones didn't have feelings; they couldn't hurt like this.

"When I reached home, I had every intention of seeing my promise to Clemmie through and remained firm about it for weeks. But my da eventually changed my mind. He was angry that I'd fallen in love with an Englishwoman—and one below our social class to boot. He wanted me to marry his partner's daughter, as had been arranged. I was weak and fearful of being cut off—as he'd told me he would do if I were to cross him as Katie had. So I did as he wanted. I married Anna. Ten months later I received a letter from Clemmie—the last of the four she'd sent asking when I was coming for her."

His voice had deepened, and Charlotte had a sickening premonition of what was coming.

"She told me she'd given birth to our child—a girl named Charleigh—and that her parents had thrown her out. She was writing to me for help. It was the first I'd learned that I was a father."

Michael looked away, as if ashamed. "I didn't tell anyone aboot the letter. Clemmie had become a shadow in me mind, a bittersweet interlude of me youth. I sent her money, then wrote to her and told her I was married, and that she shouldn't write me again." Emotion choked his voice. "It was a cowardly thing, I know, but I was afraid Anna would discover my deceit or my father would make good his threat and write me out of his will. . . . I am not proud of the man I was."

He looked up then. "When we discovered Anna would never be able to have children, I told her about you. She almost left me when she realized what I'd done—and to me own daughter. Turning me back on me own blood.

"I looked for you, Charleigh. I had detectives in London and the surrounding villages search for you. I wanted to find you, to bring you home to me and raise you as me own. But Clemmie had disappeared with you, and no one could find her."

Bitterness rose inside Charlotte, putting a bite to her words. "Your detectives looked in the wrong places. My mum was a prostitute on the seedy side of London."

Intense pain flashed across Michael's face. "Oh, Lass, I'm

so sorry. . . . Was?" he questioned, as though just hearing her words.

Charlotte gave a stiff nod. "I discovered she had died shortly after I left with Eric. He told me the news on my eighteenth birthday." She could still remember his indifferent words and how they'd pierced her heart.

Michael slowly shook his head, his eyes sliding shut. "I'm so sorry. So much pain I've caused. . .so much pain."

Hot tears threatened. Charlotte spoke the first thing that came to mind, trying to keep the tears at bay. "I remember Mum had an oval locket with a rose engraved on the front. She hid it and only brought it out occasionally. She never let me see what was inside. Giles, the tavern keeper, found it. He took it from her and sold it."

"It had a lock of me hair and me picture inside," Michael said, his words thin. "I gave it to her before I left for America."

A few of the tears Charlotte had tried to keep back spilled out. Her lower lip trembled, and she balled her fists in her lap until the nails bit into her palms. She raised her chin, regarding him with stony indifference. This was the man who'd made her mum wet her pillow with tears night after night, who'd abandoned her and hadn't cared a thing about his daughter. No wonder her mum had never told her about him. . . . She could almost hate him for what he'd done.

Michael slowly rose from the chair and walked toward her, his face a mask of longing mixed with pain and remorse. He knelt before her, covering her fists with his large hands. His eyes implored her not to turn away.

"After I found the Lord three years ago, I begged Him to let me somehow right the wrong I'd done, the wrong that ate into me soul every day," he said softly. "I knew you'd probably never want to see me after what I did to your mum—to you—but I begged Him to let me find you, to help you in any way I could. I thought His silence meant I must serve a penance for my sin."

Tears again filled his eyes, and he lowered his head to her

lap. "God brought you to me, Charleigh, I'm sure of it. He answered me prayer. It was no accident that you met Myra or came to Larkin's Glen. Forgive me, Daughter. Please forgive me for all the pain I've caused."

Charlotte stared at his bent head, holding back, bitterness warring with the desire to call this man her papa. She'd always wanted a father but had been resigned to the fact that since she was spawned in sin, she didn't deserve one. Her heart ached from his rejection of her and her mum. Yet. . . had what Michael done been any worse than what she'd done in her pretense with him? He had forgiven her. Could she do any less? He said he'd searched for her; and these past months she'd grown close to him and had seen evidence of the remorse he carried—not knowing it was connected with her in any way. . .his daughter.

Slowly, like the petals of a rose unfurling, intense longing rose inside her, and the anger and bitterness seeped away. She unfolded one of her fists that he had moistened with his tears and moved it to clasp the hand covering hers. "I forgive you."

Her soft words brought his head up, and he stared into her eyes, as if seeking assurance that she meant what she had said. With a gruff cry of thanks to God, Michael threw his arms around her.

🙚

Stewart could only stare in stunned amazement at the two people he loved most in the world as they cried tears of healing mixed with remorse and held each other tight. Slowly he rose from the chair and left the room, closing the door with a soft click behind him.

Mrs. Manning approached with a tray bearing a medicine bottle and a glass of water. "It's time for Mr. Larkin's tonic."

Stewart stared at her, still feeling as if he were in some sort of stupor.

"Please move aside, Mr. Lyons," she tried again, her tone impatient.

"Tonic?" A slow smile spread across his face. "I highly

doubt he will need that sort of tonic tonight. . .if ever again. Let him be, Mrs. Manning. He's found the best tonic there is." Winking at the baffled housekeeper, he strode to the door, whistling as he went out.

&

A week later, Stewart looked toward the front of the church, pride and admiration for Charleigh threatening to cost him his vest buttons. She'd gone up to the front during the altar call to publicly proclaim Jesus Christ as her Lord and Savior. Afterward she faced the people, and, with tears running down her face, told them of Eric and her deceit in pretending to be Myra. Finally, she asked their forgiveness. Immediately Michael took his place by her side and told the astonished church members a condensed version of his past wrong, then presented Charleigh as his daughter. Sniffles could be heard all over the room.

Tears ran down the pastor's cheeks as he faced his congregation. Stewart noticed that even the flinty Mrs. Cosgrove dabbed at her eyes with a handkerchief.

"My friends," the pastor said, his voice wavering, "what you've heard today is evidence of God's unconditional love and mercy. Though we may not understand why storms come into our lives ·or why the innocent are made to suffer, we can be assured that God's timing is perfect and His plan is above any men can fathom. Through a series of startling and tragic circumstances, God proved ever faithful. Once we submit ourselves to Him, He brings good from the bad and irons out the wrinkles—as He did in bringing this father, our friend Michael, his long-lost daughter, who lived an ocean away. And though God may not always answer our prayers with a miracle, such as the one you've heard today, rest assured: When we are obedient to His will, God always steps in and works good in our lives."

He turned to Charleigh, a smile on his face. "Charleigh Larkin, may I be the first to welcome you to the fold as my new sister in Christ." He shook her hand, then hugged her.

One by one, the congregation rose from their seats and went forward to welcome the newest member of their family. Stewart also rose and moved to the front.

Charleigh was hugged, patted on the back, and welcomed with smiles. Several people told her that her testimony had given them a boost of faith so that they now believed God could work the impossible in their own lives and painful situations concerning family members.

When it was Stewart's turn, he took both her hands in his and looked down at her, his eyes soft. "I am so proud of you."

Charleigh smiled, but Stewart discerned a flicker of uneasiness in her eyes. "I need to talk to you afterward."

He experienced a mingling of apprehension mixed with anticipation. Ever since Michael had found his daughter, he'd spent every hour of every day with her, and Stewart had been left out in the cold. Though he understood and was happy for the two reunited family members, Stewart couldn't help but feel a little jealous, because Charleigh never had time for him anymore. The look she now gave him was solemn, and Stewart felt a foreboding of what was to come.

"How about a picnic?" he said, forcing the smile to remain on his face.

She nodded, then turned to accept a hug from Amanda.

"I'm sorry you had to go through all those bad things, but I'm glad you found your papa," the little girl said as she looped her arms around Charleigh's neck. "And I'm glad you asked Jesus into your heart, too."

"So am I, Sweetie," Charleigh murmured. "So am I."

Stewart walked outside to wait, forcing down the anxiety that had cropped up at the determined look in Charleigh's eyes.

❧

"You can't be serious," Stewart said, voice low. His whole body tensed, and he sat up straighter on the grassy slope, alarmed by what Charleigh had just shared with him.

"I am." Her green eyes were steady.

"But, but that would be like slitting your own throat!" His

mouth narrowed with resolve. "I won't let you do it."

"You're the one who said criminals should be punished for their crimes—no matter their reasons for doing so."

Her soft words bludgeoned him. "Things have changed," he insisted. "You've changed. You're a different person than you were."

"Yes, you're right. I am different. I've spent most of my life in fear—afraid of my life at the tavern, afraid of Eric, afraid of being discovered when I played Myra. I'm tired of running, and I know I won't find peace until I go back to England and turn myself over to Scotland Yard. I've prayed about it, and I believe this is what God wants me to do."

Frustrated, Stewart swiped a hand along the back of his neck. "And how does Michael feel about this? Have you told him?"

"Yes. He reacted a lot like you at first, but when I explained my reasons, he understood and said he would support me. He can relate to the deep need to right a wrong." She gave him a slight smile, but Stewart didn't smile back.

Restless, he shot up from the ground and walked a few feet away from her. He heard the rustle of her dress as she rose and moved behind him.

"When do you leave?" he asked, his voice resigned.

"In a week."

"What?" Stewart spun to face her. She stood close, and he grabbed her shoulders. "Charleigh, don't do this. God has forgiven you for your crimes. You don't have to go back to England. Think of us. . . . I want to marry you. That's what that money I gave Eric was for—to buy you an engagement ring."

Her eyes widened at this admission, and tears came to them, but she shook her head. "Don't you see, Stewart? I don't want the past to come between us. As a lawyer, surely you can understand why I must do this. I can't hide forever. The only way I can let go of the past is to face it."

"You realize they may send you to prison?"

"Yes." Her reply was whisper soft.

He wrapped his arms around her, hauling her close.

"Thunderation! Do you have any idea what you're asking of me, Woman? You're asking me to let you go, possibly never to see you again, to—"

"But don't you see?" she interrupted, her cheek against his tweed jacket. "It's the only way we can really be free to love one another. Otherwise, my past would always be there to interfere and steal from us."

Her words rocked him, and he moved away a fraction so he could look down at her face. "Love one another. . .? Charleigh Larkin, did you just say you loved me?"

She hesitated, then gave a slow nod. "I think I have for some time, ever since—"

Her words were cut off as his mouth came down on hers in a poignant kiss full of longing tinged with desperation. When he broke away, his hand went to the back of her head, and he closed his eyes, breathing in her sweet rose scent. A thick tendril of hair slipped from its pin and dangled over his fingers. How could he ever let her go?

"All right," he breathed against her temple, after some time had elapsed. "If you must return to England, I'm going with you."

She shook her head, dazed. "You can't."

"Why can't I?"

"Because. . .because you have clients here that depend on you."

"I'll refer them to someone else."

"Stewart, I'd rather you didn't. . . ."

"I'm not losing sight of you again."

"Papa has said he will come with me. I won't be alone."

He shook his head, frustrated. "Charleigh, don't try to change my mind. I'm going."

She looked at him, uncertainty filling her eyes. He took her hand, ignoring the thread of doubt that assailed him. Didn't she want him with her? Was there something else she was hiding?

"Come," he said, his voice gruff. "Let's go tell Michael of my decision."

thirteen

"No, Lad."

Michael's words were soft, but the impact of them shook Stewart, and he swiveled away from the window. "No?" He stared at Michael incredulously. "What do you mean, no?"

"It wouldn't be a good idea. And if you give it more thought, you would see that, too."

Stewart began to pace, the old hound following him with weary brown eyes from his post on the hearth. Stewart had been certain that Michael would not only endorse his idea to accompany them to London, but be excited about it as well. Michael's sober countenance irritated him. "Well, I have decided. And whether or not you're in favor—"

"Stop yer wanderin'; sit down a minute and listen." Michael waited until Stewart reluctantly took a seat across from him. "Would you throw away your profession? All you've worked so hard to establish? Who would be takin' care of the people's needs? That weasel, Harlem Stodges? This town needs a good lawyer, one who has the people at heart—not their money."

Stewart looked away, uneasy. "If necessary, I would stay in London only a short time. . . ."

"And what of Trevor Ingles? Who would take his case?"

Stewart closed his eyes when he thought of the young farmer who was fighting a wealthy landowner determined to push him off his adjoining twenty acres—and using every dirty trick in the book to do it.

"I wouldn't be gone long."

"Stewart, listen to me. I know you care for me daughter, and I'm highly in favor of a union between the two of you— in fact, it's me fondest desire. But how would you support

Charleigh if you leave your responsibilities behind? When you do come back to America, how many of the townspeople do you think would trust you with their cases, knowing you left poor Trevor in the lurch?"

Stewart felt the decision slipping away from him, and, desperate, he tried to hold on. "I love her, Michael. Regardless of her past and all she's done, I love her."

Michael's eyes softened. "I know, Lad, and I tink she loves you as well. Stay here and prepare your home for her. Build your reputation as a trusted lawyer. Build a future for the two of ye to share."

Frustration filled Stewart when he realized Michael was right. Still, he remained fixed. "I don't want to lose her."

"If it be God's will for you to be together, you won't." When Stewart remained silent, Michael continued. "I cannot force you to stay, Lad. I can only advise you to do what is right. You wouldn't be happy with anything less."

Stewart didn't reply, only gave an abrupt nod.

"Besides," Michael said, his tone lightening as he moved to pat the old hound's head. "I was hoping you would take care of Methuselah for me while I'm gone. He'll be lonely without me."

A tapping at the door preceded Charleigh, who walked into the room. She looked tense, uncertain, and Stewart immediately rose and went to her side.

"Are you all right?"

She nodded, though the smile she gave him was thin. "I was just realizing how much I'll miss it here. . . . And yet, just a few days ago, I never thought I'd see Larkin's Glen again. So much has happened in such a short time."

Her words cut Stewart to the quick. He realized how swiftly a week would fly by and realized also, thanks to Michael's logic, that he must stay behind. If only there was something he could do!

Sudden inspiration came to him, and he blinked, wondering why he hadn't thought of it sooner. "Charleigh, I must tend to an urgent matter now, but I will return tonight."

He deposited a quick kiss on her cheek, ignoring her startled eyes, and hurried out the door.

❧

On the day of their departure, Charlotte stood and stared at the garden in full bloom, conflicting emotions waging war inside her. She knew without a doubt that the Lord was showing her that she must return to England. But now that the day had arrived, fear threatened to strangle her and sway her from her decision. She knelt at the lattice bench, rested clasped hands on the iron seat, and prayed in her secret place one last time.

"Lord, I am so frightened. Give me courage to do what You want me to do. Please give me the strength I need. I am so weak and so very afraid. . . ." She squeezed her eyes shut, pressing her fingers tighter and bringing her clasped hands up under her chin.

Do not fear, my daughter. The soft words caressed her spirit like a refreshing breeze. *I am with you always, and I will give you everything you need. . . .*

Charlotte looked up at the robin's egg blue sky, tears of gratitude filling her eyes. A rustle in the grass brought her head around.

Mrs. Manning looked at her with narrowed eyes. "Mr. Larkin told me to tell you the carriage is waiting, Miss Charleigh."

Charlotte wondered if she would ever grow accustomed to that name again. "Thank you," she said as she rose from the ground.

Before she could sweep past the housekeeper, however, the old woman laid a hand on her arm. Charlotte turned her head in surprise. The housekeeper looked flustered, an unusual emotion for her.

"Is it true? Are you really his daughter?"

Charlotte gave an abrupt nod, mentally preparing for the woman's censure. Mrs. Manning hesitated, clearly undecided about something, then slipped a hand inside her apron pocket, pulled out a pair of wire-rimmed glasses, and propped them on her nose.

Charlotte watched in astonishment as the squinting eyes widened to normal size and scanned Charlotte's face. "I always thought you favored Mr. Larkin's mother, but could never tell for sure. Now I see that you do!"

She smiled, her eyes kind, and Charlotte was taken aback. All this time she'd thought the woman suspicious and antagonistic toward her—and she was only nearsighted!

Charlotte returned her smile, feeling like a fool. "Thank you, Mrs. Manning. You couldn't have paid me a higher compliment."

"Charleigh?"

At Michael's gruff voice, the housekeeper hastily snatched the glasses from her nose and stuffed them back into her pocket. "Well, I'll be wishing you godspeed and a hasty return to Larkin's Glen," she muttered before hurrying past Michael, back into the house.

"Are ye ready to go, Lass? Stewart is waiting."

The seriousness of the moment swamped Charlotte once more, and she nodded, turned, and surveyed the garden one last time. Would she ever see it again? Here she had found the Lord and spent many precious hours with Him. Here she had found a measure of peace and the will to go on. And here she had talked with her earthly father and had grown to know him. . . .

She sighed, strode toward him, and put a hand on his arm. "I'm ready, Papa."

Michael's eyes sparkled with happiness at the name, but his countenance remained solemn. He, too, knew that the next few weeks would be the hardest of their lives.

≈

Charlotte sat on her narrow bunk in the dank cell, alone, and pondered the last week. When she'd walked into Scotland Yard—leaving her frustrated father outside in the carriage and telling him she must go in unaccompanied by him—then announced her crimes to the young man at the desk, he'd looked at her as if she were daft. Charlotte wryly assumed such a thing had never happened at the famous agency. Certainly not many criminals willingly turned themselves over to be punished.

At first the constable had treated her with shocked surprise and uncertainty. But when she'd given him names and dates and mentioned Lord Appleby, he'd consulted his coworkers, and they'd transported her to a holding cell, containing a few women of low reputation, while they investigated.

Something strange happened while she was there. Something she couldn't explain or understand. Despite the women's insults and coarse talk concerning her "hoity-toity clothes and airs," Charlotte felt pity for these women, whose crimes were no worse than hers, and wanted them to have what she'd so recently found. Later that night, Charlotte worked up enough courage to begin telling them about the Lord—but she was cut off by loud cursing and threats.

"Leave it be, Duckie," a thin woman with scraggly dark ringlets whispered to her later, after joining her in a corner of the room Charlotte had taken. "Ye won' be gettin' far with the likes o' them."

Charlotte turned to look at her fellow prisoner, who'd been the first to show kindness. The girl looked younger than Charlotte. Her complexion was pasty, the paint rubbed off her cheeks in places, and her hollow dark eyes held secrets better left unspoken. Charlotte recognized the look in those eyes.

"I'm Charlotte—I mean Charleigh," she corrected.

The girl hesitated. "Me name's Darcy."

"Why are you here, Darcy?" Charlotte asked.

The girl shook her head, her expression going blank again. "Why is any of us here? Sure as not for the scenery." She gave a hollow laugh. "An' I don' expect any of us walked in one day an' gave ourselves up, either."

"I did."

"Yer pullin' me leg." Darcy's eyes widened when Charlotte remained silent. "You are, aren't you?"

"No, Darcy. Before I gave my life to Christ, I did a lot of bad things, and now I'm paying for my crimes. I know God has forgiven me, but justice must be served nonetheless."

Dark brows bunched together, Darcy studied her incredulously. At last she shook her head. "Yer a strange bird, all right. . . ."

Charlotte only gave her a weak smile.

A few mornings later, she was surprised when a tall, well-dressed young man with blond hair and sideburns came to the cell. His eyes instantly focused on Charlotte, and the next thing she knew, she was alone with him in another room, as bare as the one she'd left.

"Stewart Lyons wrote me," he explained as soon as the guard had closed the door. "We've been good friends for years—since I met him in London. He asked me to look after you. Lionel Humphries, at your service." He took off his hat and gave a deep bow, his dark blue eyes twinkling.

"Look after me?" Charlotte repeated; she was confused, yet thankful for his likable personality. After several days in the crowded cell, Charlotte appreciated his cheerful countenance.

"I'm to represent your case."

"You're a barrister?"

He lifted a brow at her incredulous tone, and her face went hot. "I assure you, Miss Larkin, I can be very serious and persuasive when the need arises. I especially am interested in the unusual and extraordinary—and your case definitely fits that category, from what Stewart wrote in the letter. Now, shall we begin?"

He sat in a chair across from her, and for the next hour Charlotte told him everything, with him inserting a question or two now and then. Later that day, she was moved to a different cell, this one private, and even given a Bible upon request.

Charlotte looked down at the open pages now, a soft smile on her lips. She missed Darcy's company, regardless of the short time that had passed since she'd made her acquaintance, and wished she could have somehow gotten through to her. But this time alone in the cell had taught Charlotte something important.

She now understood the mystery of the words "in the secret place." They didn't refer to a beautiful garden in full bloom; nor were they only words scrawled at the bottom of a peculiar painting hanging on a parlor wall, as she'd once thought. Rather, the secret place referred to time spent in the presence of the Most High God. Time spent conversing and listening to the Lord—through Scripture and through prayer. Though all around her might be stark and frightening—as represented by winter in the painting—time spent with God, abiding in Him, caused winter to fade until she basked in the sunshine of His glory. His presence. His secret place.

Her wondering gaze lifted to the barred window. Streams of golden sunshine poured through the openings of the steel bars and made a pool of shimmering light on the dirty stone floor.

No matter if she was sentenced to life in prison, no one could ever take away her freedom. Her freedom in Christ. Like Saint Paul, she'd learned the secret of being content in any situation.

Yes, she missed Stewart. And she was thankful for their short time together. But the more she pondered his parting words to her and remembered her foolish slip of the tongue regarding her feelings for him, the more she realized their love could never be. Stewart was a respected lawyer, and Charlotte was a former criminal. A life with her would put his career in jeopardy, she was certain. How many people would trust an attorney whose wife had led a life of crime?

Charlotte shook her head sadly at the thought and prayed the Lord would remove her desire to become Stewart's wife.

Two sets of hollow footsteps echoed through the corridor, coming her way, and she directed her surprised gaze to the cell door. Her father had visited many times already, but these steps were lighter and faster. They weren't heavy like his.

The metallic sound of a key screeched in the lock and the door swung inward. She stared in puzzlement at the short, portly man in expensive attire who stared back at her from pitiless gray eyes. His stern expression sent shivers down her spine, and she furrowed her brow in confusion as she stood and faced him, his cold manner putting her at once on the defensive.

"Come now, Mademoiselle Fontaneau," he scoffed, his stance indignant as he entered her cell. "Surely you remember me?"

Charlotte intently studied the silver-haired man before her. Gasping, her eyes widened in recognition, and her knees felt as if they might give way.

"Lord Appleby," she whispered.

A feeling of unreality consumed Charlotte as she looked at the dead man. Only he wasn't dead. She must have voiced her thoughts, for he sneered and said, "No, I'm not dead. You and your brother's scheme didn't succeed after all. It was advantageous for me that a fishing boat was nearby and they investigated upon hearing the splash—after your brother pushed my unconscious body into the Thames once he had robbed me."

Charlotte only stared, unable to frame words as she slowly sank to her bunk.

"When news hit the papers of a woman turning herself in to Scotland Yard, I was curious. But when a constable contacted me, claiming she told them she was responsible for my death, I decided to see for myself." He sneered at her again. "I'm delighted to see you where you belong at last and will do my utmost to see your brother rot in jail as well!"

Charlotte made no defensive reply to his vehement words; she just regarded him sadly. "I can never express to you just how wretched I've felt for what we did, Lord Appleby," she said at last. "I'm relieved to see you didn't die." She offered a feeble smile. "You don't know how relieved."

His look slowly changed from loathing to bewilderment to

indecision. Then his face clouded with anger again. "Don't think you can sweet-talk your way out of this, Mademoiselle!"

"I'm not doing any such thing," she responded softly. "I only seek your forgiveness. Scotland Yard didn't apprehend me. I turned myself over to them—remember? I'm well aware that I must pay for my crimes and intend to do so."

His brows bunched in perplexity. He shook his head as though his thoughts were muddled. Some of the fire left his eyes, though the frown remained on his face.

"Why did you do it, Charlotte?" he asked, his voice low, almost pleading. "I thought you were different. . . ." His words trailed away at the pained look on her face.

She shook her head. "My reasons are of no matter now."

"Don't you even desire freedom?" he asked, astonished. He was confused that she offered no excuses for her prior behavior, as he'd expected. Quiet strength seemed to flow from her, a calm he'd never seen in anyone, leaving him curious. She little resembled the woman he'd met a year ago. "What is there about you that is so different?"

She hesitated, then smiled.

৯

Stewart pored over his closing briefs, rubbing one bleary eye with two fingers. The case of Rodham Gleason versus Trevor Ingles was finally closed. Samuel, an orphaned lad of fourteen, had been caught setting fire to Trevor's fields at night, and he confessed that Gleason had paid him to do it. Further investigation had led to others' confessions, several checks for services rendered with Gleason's name on them, and more incriminating bits of evidence. Gleason was now in jail where he belonged—though with his crooked lawyer searching for loopholes, the length of his stay was impossible to determine.

Stewart's gaze went to the rain-spattered window. And what of Charleigh? Lionel had wired him that he was doing what he could to hurry her trial and that it should be coming up any day. Stewart had received four letters from Michael, two from Lionel, and only one from her. His gaze went to the smudged letter that he'd read many times these past six months.

She had exulted that Lord Appleby was alive and had come to visit her three times in her cell before Michael had posted her bail; at first he'd been full of righteous indignation, then he expressed curiosity about the change in her. "And," she'd written, "though he hasn't yet accepted Christ and remains aloof concerning the gospel, his hunger for it is evident in the questions he asks. I think his salvation is at hand."

Stewart frowned at Charleigh's strangely impersonal letter. Not once had she mentioned her love for him or anything the least bit intimate. Just who was this Lord Appleby? Was the interest he had in Charleigh merely spiritual? Stewart doubted it. If the man had no designs on Charleigh, why would he drop the charges concerning her, as Lionel had written? She and Eric had robbed the man and tried to murder him, for pity's sake! Not that Stewart wasn't relieved that she now only faced various theft charges—he was—but why had the man done it? What did he hope to gain from his generous deed? Charleigh's love?

A tapping sounded at the door.

"What is it?" Stewart growled.

His housekeeper entered, a frown on her face. "Still at it I see," she said with obvious disapproval. "Your dinner is getting cold. . . ."

"Thank you, Irma," he said in clipped tones, "but I'm not hungry. Did you want something?"

She shook her head, "tsk-tsking" him, and pulled an envelope from her apron pocket. "Telegram arrived."

Stewart stared, then grabbed the yellow rectangle from her fingers and tore into the envelope with haste:

Trial over. Stop. Charleigh sentenced to three years in reformatory. Stop. Letter to follow.

Lionel

Stewart stared at the paper, unbelieving, and then crumpled

it in one hand, his eyes sliding shut. "Pack my bag," he told the startled housekeeper. "I'm leaving for London tonight."

"Mr. Lyons—"

"Now, Irma!" His commanding voice shook the room and she hurried out the door, unaccustomed to his angry tone.

Stewart stared after her, his thoughts in turmoil. "Why, God? Why Charleigh?" He gave a cynical laugh, the irony of the situation threatening to tear him apart inside. All these years he'd fought to see the guilty put behind bars, to see justice met. Now justice was being served. . .and he abhorred it.

How many of those who had required his counsel over the years had been the pawn of evil men like Eric? Stewart sobered as he remembered one desperate woman who'd come to him—a widow with two children. But he'd turned her away because, when he looked at her, he was reminded of his cousin's wife and was certain of her guilt. He was often praised for his integrity and inclination to help those in distress, reputed to have a heart for the people. Lies, all lies.

He'd never sought justice. What he desired had been revenge.

It had been he who had found Steven hanging by a rope in his study. It had been he who cut down his childhood friend and cousin, tears clouding his eyes—and sworn he would find the woman responsible for leaving Steven with no desire to live. The woman who'd taken all his money and disappeared as swiftly as a thieving fox escapes to its den. Yet Stewart had never found her. From that day on, every case he'd taken had been his way of trying to right a personal wrong, the wrong done to Steven. And then he'd met Charleigh.

Stewart closed his eyes and dipped his head into his hand, massaging his forehead with his fingers. Had he known of her crimes from the start, Stewart doubted he would have treated her with compassion, but likely would have turned her over to the police. Yet, in growing to care for her, and intrigued by her secretiveness and vulnerability, he'd opened himself to see what he couldn't see before: that sometimes justice should be tempered with mercy. Sometimes the guilty committed crimes out of fear, not knowing a better way; they needed someone to show them the right way. It had taken the imprisonment of the woman he loved to open his eyes to the truth. And he determined never to forget this night.

❧

"Michael, why are we here?" Stewart impatiently dodged a large puddle in the muddy road, walking beside the older man, between the decaying tenements. "Where are we going?"

Michael had acted strangely since meeting him at the dock, though he hadn't seemed the least bit surprised by Stewart's arrival in London. Stewart had already been told by Lionel that permission would have to be sought for him to visit Charleigh; Stewart swallowed his disappointment and determined to wait. At least Lionel had told him the good news that, upon investigating, Charleigh's marriage to Eric was found unquestionably to be fraudulent. Stewart had wanted to be certain, not trusting Eric's word.

Michael now seemed absentminded yet determined, as though his mind were on something of great importance. He glanced at Stewart, clearly undecided, then gave an abrupt nod, never breaking stride. "Something about Charleigh's confession at Larkin's Glen bothered me, though I couldn't determine what it was. I've been so caught up in Charleigh, I've had little time to think upon the matter. But now that the trial is over, and there's little more I can do except visit her as they allow me, I've pondered the situation."

Stewart listened with a keen ear as he hastily sidestepped a pile of horse manure. The stench of rot and filth permeated the air in this poor part of London. The strong smell of fish intermingled, and Stewart saw with some surprise that they were nearing the wharf.

"Charleigh said that Eric was the one to tell her of her mother's death. I questioned her later, and she told me she never once visited Clemmie's grave." In his excitement, Michael's pace increased, and Stewart was hard-pressed to keep up, even though he was long-legged.

"Now just suppose, mind ye, Eric had lied—being the controller he was," Michael hastily continued. "Just from the little Charleigh told me, I wouldn't put it past the scoundrel to do such a thing, and in so doing, gain complete control of me daughter. If she thought him the only person of note left in her life, it would trap her further in his snare. For who then would she run to?"

Stewart smiled. "I think you missed your calling, Michael. You should have been a detective. But why would Charleigh want to return to her mother? Her life at the tavern was a hell in itself."

"Aye, Lad, but you're forgetting one thing. Eric may not have known this—their courtship and phony marriage were sudden—but even if he did, he knew about her love for her mother. By cutting off the one person Charleigh cared aboot and forever removing her from Charleigh's life, Eric might have hoped to gain even more control over me daughter."

A scowl crossed Michael's face, but as they reached a narrow road intersecting the one they were on, the spark of interest lit his eyes again, and he turned left, Stewart with him. "I visited the tavern where Clemmie worked two days ago," Michael admitted. "The tavern keeper told me nothing, even ordered me out, but there was a fishmonger's wife who'd overheard our confrontation. After I left the tavern, she motioned me aside and told me that Clemmie left there two years ago, and she knew where she went. Said she'd even visited her once or twice."

Michael intently scanned the buildings as he talked, then abruptly stopped, putting a hand to Stewart's arm. "Here we are." He looked soulfully at his friend. "Soon we shall know the truth."

Nothing more was said as the two men walked up the decaying stoop of the old tenement, and Michael put his hand to the weathered door.

fourteen

"My mother is alive?" Charleigh echoed in disbelief. She gripped the coarse wood handle of the hoe tightly. The color seeped from her cheeks, and her face went chalk white.

Stewart took her arm, wanting to lead her away from the vegetable garden and to the wooden bench that sat on the other side of the large farmhouse, away from the all-seeing eyes of one of the matrons who ran the reformatory. He'd been allotted only fifteen minutes and wanted to spend every moment he could with Charleigh. He only wished he could take her in his arms, but the penetrating dark eyes watching them clearly made that impossible.

A young dark-headed girl, in the stark gray uniform dress all the inmates wore, took Charleigh's hoe from her tight grip. "Go sit down, Luv, before you fall down."

"Thank you, Darcy," Charleigh murmured. She walked beside Stewart as if she were in a trance. "Tell me," she breathed, once they'd settled on the rickety bench. "Tell me everything."

Stewart paused. He could never tell her of the rat-infested, decaying tenement that housed her mother's spare single room. Nor could he tell her of the emaciated figure with snarled, graying hair they'd found on the dirty cot. When they knocked and entered, she'd stared at them at first with trepidation, then confusion, finally telling them in a weak voice that she no longer took clients due to her sickness.

"Clemmie." Michael had looked at her with agonized eyes as he slowly approached, his voice wavering with emotion. "Clemmie, it's Michael."

She shook her head in puzzlement—then horror replaced the blank look on her hollow features. "Michael," she rasped, as she tried to move further back into the bedding. "Go away." She began to cough. "I'm not fit. . . . Please, just go."

He ignored her soft pleading and knelt at her bedside. "I've come to beg your forgiveness, Clemmie, though I know I'm not deservin' of it. . . ."

At first she'd been resistant, then resigned. Tears came even to Stewart's eyes as the two at the bedside quietly spoke and cried, and Michael moved to gently hold her. At that moment Stewart had felt like an interloper, though he was certain they'd forgotten his presence in the room.

"Stewart?"

Charleigh's impatient voice brought him back to the present. He regarded her solemnly, noting her anxious green eyes. "Eric lied to you, Charleigh. Your mother never sold you to him."

Shocked confusion marred her brow. "Then why. . .?"

"Your mother is a very sick woman. She's been sick a long time but didn't want to worry you, what with everything you had to endure at the tavern. Eric discovered her condition and offered to pay for a doctor and medicine. Whether he did it from a guilty conscience or as one uncharacteristic act of kindness or to sway your mother in allowing you to marry him, I don't know, though I suspect the latter."

"Then she's truly alive?" Tears filled her eyes. "I can scarce believe it. . . . But—but you said she's ill?"

Stewart looked away. "Michael took her to a hospital that very day, and she's receiving the best of care."

Charlotte studied him, feeling as if he were withholding something from her. "And?"

He expelled a loud breath, his dark brows bunching together in uncertainty.

"Tell me, Stewart. I have a right to know."

He looked her way, his eyes sad. "Charleigh, your mother has been sick for some time. The doctor said she's in the last stages of the disease. . . ."

"So. . .what you're telling me is that I've found my mother

only to lose her again?" Emotion colored her voice, and she swallowed hard, praying for control. "And I may never see her. She can't come here, and I can't go there. . . ." Her eyes slid shut, then flew open again. She gripped his arm.

"Then you must tell her, Stewart," she said, her voice steady and determined. "You must tell her about the way that leads to salvation through Jesus Christ and help her find it before it's too late. Will you do this for me?"

Stewart brushed a tear from her cheek. "If Michael hasn't already, you know I will. He visits her often. He's there right now."

"I'm glad for that, anyway." She bit her inside lower lip to try to stop more tears from following.

"I wish I could take you in my arms and kiss your tears away," he said very softly, his voice intense. She stiffened, and he frowned. "What's wrong, Charleigh?"

She pulled at the fingers of her hand that lay in the folds of her skirt. "Stewart, I've been thinking. . . ."

When she didn't go on, he inclined his head, his serious gaze unwavering. She averted her eyes.

"Perhaps we shouldn't see one another again. Three years is a long time, and I'm certain you could find someone more worthy to—"

"No," he cut her off. By his riveting gaze and the way he suddenly grasped her hands and leaned closer toward her, Charlotte felt certain he would kiss her, regardless of their public surroundings. However, he refrained from doing so, only giving her hands another tight squeeze. "No."

"But Stewart, your practice. . ."

"Get all foolish thoughts like that out of your head right now, Woman. You are more important to me than my practice. I'd rather move to another town and start over than live my life without you. But I don't believe I will have to do either of those things."

She shook her head slowly, not knowing what to say.

Worry knit his brow. "But maybe I'm assuming too much?

Perhaps your love belongs to someone else? Someone like Lord Appleby, for instance?"

Despite the serious moment, Charlotte couldn't help but let out a small, incredulous laugh. "Lord Appleby?"

"You wrote much about him in your letter."

At his woebegone look, Charlotte managed a smile. "Lord Appleby is a lonely widower who is older than my father. Though I'm concerned about his spirit, I'm not interested in a relationship with him." At the sudden light in Stewart's eyes, she hastened to add, "But that doesn't mean I think there's hope for you and me, either."

"Do you love me, Charleigh?"

"I wouldn't make a good lawyer's wife. I've never been on the right side of the law. . . ."

"Do you love me, Charleigh?" He took her hand in a gentle clasp, running his thumb over her dirt-stained fingers and sending her heart into spasms.

"People will talk. . . ."

"Do you love me, Charleigh?" he asked, softer this time, his other hand moving to cup her cheek, his face moving closer.

"It would never work," she whispered.

"Charleigh. . .do you love me?"

"Yes," she admitted the moment before Stewart's lips touched hers. The kiss was brief, but full of promise, and sent Charlotte's pulse racing.

"That's all I wanted to know," he said huskily, tracing her features with his eyes. His mouth curved in a soft smile. "You're forgetting one thing in all your arguments for why it could never work between us. And that is, what's the Lord's will in this? Have you sought Him concerning us?"

A thickset matron rounded the corner, arms crossed, the expression on her face unbending.

Stewart gave a resigned sigh. "I have to go now, Charleigh, but I want you to know I will wait for you. However long it takes. I believe God has shown me that you're the one He's chosen for me, but I want you to come to that knowledge as well." He kissed her fingertips, ignoring the scowling face of the matron. "There's never been anyone else, and there never will be. Three years from now, I'll be waiting, Charleigh."

Heart thumping madly, her breath caught in her throat, Charlotte watched him stride to the gate before she returned on shaky legs to her plot in the garden.

Was Stewart right? Was it God's will for them to be together?

❧

Charlotte breathed in the crisp, cool air of a New York autumn. The leaves on the trees had turned into a blaze of fiery color, leaving her awed. As her father urged the horses over the bridge, Charlotte solemnly watched a few orange leaves from a nearby tree spiral to the shimmering water below; a sudden breath of wind had freed them from their branches.

She had never gotten to see her mother again. Clemmie died almost one month to the day after Michael had found her. Charlotte was thankful that her mother had accepted the Lord the week after Michael had made contact with her, and she knew one day they would be reunited again in a place where there was no disease, or pain, or death. A smile tipped her lips at the thought of how her mother must be at this moment: young and free as the breeze, her golden hair rippling, light green eyes dancing, and laughter like tinkling bells ringing through heaven.

Though Charlotte couldn't say the past three years had gone swiftly, much had been accomplished at Turreney Farm. Besides the bone-wearying work, chapel and a half-hour of Bible study both morning and evening had been on the daily schedule. Charlotte had been a model inmate at the strict institution, sometimes eliciting special privileges for her behavior. At the front of the farmhouse she'd even been allowed to help plant roses, which the head matron favored. But the most worthwhile event at the farm had been the day, a year ago, that Darcy had come to the knowledge of Christ, with Charlotte's help.

Charlotte was sorry to leave behind her dear friend, but the longing to be with her father and Stewart crowded out any desire to remain behind. And though Europe was at war, something that struck terror in Charlotte's heart every time she thought about it—afraid America might soon join in and Stewart would go and fight—she braved the danger of sailing over hostile waters, praying God would protect her, as He had on the *Titanic*.

Her mind went to Stewart, and she puckered her brow, anxiety clouding her thoughts. Since that sunny afternoon three years ago, when he'd told her about her mother and vowed his love for her, there had been a letter every couple of months. . .dwindling in time to one a season. And then, this past year, they had stopped altogether.

Her father had explained that Stewart was extremely busy with work and had little time to write. He had planned to meet them in Manhattan. However, problems had arisen at the last moment, and he was unable to get away.

Charlotte understood. But that didn't dispel the doubt that relentlessly niggled at her mind. Had Stewart's feelings for her changed? Perhaps he'd discovered that she'd been right all along and now believed a future between them could never work out. Charlotte still wasn't certain it was God's will for them to be together. At the farm, whenever she'd found a rare moment to enter the secret place and have private time with the Lord, He'd seemed strangely silent concerning the matter of a future with Stewart, regardless of her pleas. Yet God had never taken away the love she felt for the man nor the desire to be his wife.

Though it had been a long time since she'd been in the area, Charlotte noticed when her father didn't take the turnoff. Puzzled, she looked his way. "Where are we going? This isn't the way to Larkin's Glen."

He stared straight ahead, though she thought she detected a twinkle in the blue eyes. His skin glowed with health and he'd put on a little weight, no sign of illness about him. She felt thankful that he obviously was no longer tormented by the past.

"I've orders to take you somewhere first," he explained.

Charlotte stifled a groan. She was exhausted from the trip and hoped the ladies of the church hadn't planned a welcoming party this soon.

"Orders? Papa, I really don't think—"

"Hush, Charleigh," he said with a smile, "lest you cause me to reveal too much and ruin the surprise."

Charlotte settled back and crossed her arms over her chest in resignation. So, she was right. A party had been arranged.

She watched as Michael took another turnoff, and she vaguely remembered being down this road before. A huge, familiar farmhouse with dormer windows and an added wing stood at one end, but what caught her attention immediately was the sign next to the white picket fence: LYONS'S REFUGE.

Head jerking to the side, Charlotte turned huge eyes her father's way, but he ignored her as he drove through the open gate toward the rear of the house, and she turned her attention back to the surrounding pastureland.

Two lads, Charlotte guessed them to be about sixteen, were busy mending the fence in one part of the field. Another boy, much younger, walked toward the house carrying a large bucket.

As she watched, Mrs. Manning opened the door and called to the boy, "Hurry up, Steven! Irma needs those apples today!" She turned at the sound of the wagon, threw up her hands, and called into the house, "They're here, Mr. Lyons! They're here!"

Stewart came through the door, his quick stride almost a trot. His gaze locked with Charlotte's, and all former worries vanished at the love she saw glowing in his eyes.

He caught her to him before she'd put her foot to the ground. "At last," he breathed as he swung her down and brought her close, holding her as if he'd never let go. Charlotte felt all the tension leave her as she wrapped her arms around his neck and burrowed her face against his solid chest. How she had longed for this day!

Michael cleared his throat. "I'll just go on inside and see if Alice brought any of her strudel. I'm a mite hungry after that train ride." His steps crunched away.

Charlotte blinked, then looked up at Stewart. "Alice?"

"Mrs. Manning," he explained with a smile, his gaze touching upon her every feature. "A lot has happened since you went away."

"Obviously," she murmured, feeling breathless by the look in his eyes. They continued to stare at one another in silence. His hand moved to tenderly cup her face, then slowly his mouth lowered to hers.

Loud guffaws broke them apart. Startled, Charlotte turned her head. A small freckled and very dirty face observed them from behind the thick trunk of a nearby tree. Seeing he was caught, the face zipped back into place behind the tree, hidden from view again.

"Lance Ruebels," Stewart intoned in a quiet yet commanding voice, "come out from there this instant."

A pause, a rustle of leaves, then a scrawny boy of about ten shuffled out, hands in his jeans pockets. "Yessir?"

"You know better than to spy on your elders," Stewart said in the same tone of voice. "Now go see if Irma has anything for you to do to keep you out of mischief. But first, wash up."

"Yessir." His hazel eyes landed on Charlotte. "She sure is a powerful lot prettier than Irma," he said with a smirk before turning and loping to the house.

Flustered by the remark, Charlotte stared after the boy, then cut her eyes to Stewart in confusion. "Who was that?" She briefly looked toward the fence where the two boys had picked up the hammer and pail of nails and then headed for the barn. "And where do they come from?"

"That was Lance," Stewart said casually. "He's a pickpocket."

Charlotte's eyes grew wide. "Pickpocket?"

Stewart nodded. "And the two boys mending the fence are

Samuel and Brian. Samuel was caught setting fire to a field, and Brian stole food from a grocer. It wasn't a first offense for either of them. Steven, the boy carrying the vegetables, has had several charges brought against him, ranging from stealing to vandalism. But it's Joel I'm really concerned about."

Dazed, Charlotte pressed her fingertips to her temples, slowly shaking her head as she tried to make sense of his strange words. "Stealing? Vandalism? Pickpocketing? Just what is going on here, Stewart?"

"I didn't want to tell you until I knew for sure I could open one—and keep it up—but you're looking at a reform school for young criminals. We opened the first of this year, thanks to your father's funding."

Her mouth dropped open. "Reform school?" She shook her head again. "What about your practice?"

"At present I'm not taking on any new clients, though I'm still representing your father and a few others in small matters." A troubled look entered his eyes. "I had the wrong motives for becoming a lawyer, Charleigh. This is a way I can see justice served, yet help the guilty at the same time."

Charlotte furrowed her brow. "But you're such a good lawyer," she protested with a frown. "It's because of me, isn't it? You did this because people would never accept you if you had anything to do with me, since I was a criminal."

Stewart laid a forefinger across her lips. "I did this because I felt it was what the Lord wanted me to do," he corrected softly. "But if He should ever prompt me to take up my practice again, I will."

Charlotte couldn't argue with that.

A rustle of leaves from behind brought both their heads around. A young boy, possibly eleven, with white-blond hair and an angelic face, stared at them. Though there was a hardness in his blue eyes, usually only seen in those older, a beautiful smile tipped his lips as he swept off his cap and gave a deep bow. "Good day, Miss Larkin. Welcome to Lyons's Refuge."

"Good day." Charleigh was charmed by the lad, but she

noticed Stewart had gone rigid.

"Joel, you're late."

The boy shrugged carelessly. "I knocked over a pail of water while I was cleaning the stables."

Stewart searched his face, then gave an abrupt sideways nod to the house. "Go."

The boy left, after another dazzling smile directed toward Charlotte. She turned to Stewart. "Why is he here?"

His gaze held hers a moment before he answered. "His father is a con artist and taught Joel everything about the trade. Joel was caught instigating an illegal shell game and making quite a deal of money from it, too. His father is in prison."

Charlotte felt dizzy with the revelation. "Like Eric." The boy even favored him, with his good looks and flagrant charm.

"Yes," Stewart said softly. "Exactly like Eric. When the judge told me about Joel, I knew I had to help the boy any way I could and try to prevent him from turning into another Eric."

She nodded, unable to speak as thoughts of her old adversary came to her. She shivered.

"Charleigh, there's something you should know, something your father and I thought best to wait and tell you. I was going to talk to you later today, but. . ." He shook his head. "Eric is dead. I read the account in a newspaper over a year ago."

"What?" Charlotte felt her legs grow weak, and she gripped his arm for support. "Dead?"

Stewart nodded. "They found his body behind a warehouse near the wharf in Manhattan. Apparently he crossed the wrong person. There was nothing to identify him, but a dockworker overheard him tell a couple of men he was the son of a French count and give his name as Philip Rawlins—the same name you told me he used on the *Carpathia*."

Charlotte wasn't certain what she felt. Relief? Pity? Sadness?

"Are you okay?"

She nodded vaguely, her gaze going to the door. "I'm glad you're helping Joel. . .and the others."

His face lit up. "The reform is still new, and we only have five boys right now, though we have the capacity to hold twenty. Brent Thomas tutors the boys for a few hours during the day, then the rest of the time is spent working around the farm and learning to make good use of their hands and time. On Sundays I take them into town for church services."

She smiled. "I'm impressed."

His gaze locked with hers. "There's only one thing missing."

"Oh?" The soft but serious look in his eyes left her breathless.

"Only one thing that would make life complete here. . .you." He took her suddenly clammy hands in his. "Charleigh Larkin, will you marry me and work beside me to help these boys find a better way?"

Tears filled Charlotte's eyes. Reassuring peace flowed through her, and she felt as if her heavenly Father was smiling down on them from heaven. She had her answer.

"Yes, Stewart Lyons, I will."

"Thank God!" He grinned, then hauled her close and kissed her. Charlotte felt as if she might float away from happiness. She was so grateful to be alive.

"Oh, brother! They're smoochin' again," a young boy's voice screeched from the porch in disgust. "Mr. Lyons, are you ever gonna come in so's we can eat?"

Stewart broke the kiss and gave Charlotte an embarrassed grin, which she returned. Hand in hand, they moved toward the farmhouse and the brood of five boys curiously staring at them from the porch.

"Boys, this is Miss Larkin," Stewart said proudly. "She will soon be mistress of Lyons's Refuge."

Charlotte smiled. She had come home.

A Letter To Our Readers

Dear Reader:

In order that we might better contribute to your reading enjoyment, we would appreciate your taking a few minutes to respond to the following questions. We welcome your comments and read each form and letter we receive. When completed, please return to the following:

Rebecca Germany, Fiction Editor
Heartsong Presents
PO Box 719
Uhrichsville, Ohio 44683

1. Did you enjoy reading *In the Secret Place* by Pamela Griffin?
   ☐ Very much! I would like to see more books by this author!
   ☐ Moderately. I would have enjoyed it more if

   _____

   _____

   _____

2. Are you a member of **Heartsong Presents**? Yes ☐ No ☐
   If no, where did you purchase this book?_____

   _____

3. How would you rate, on a scale from 1 (poor) to 5 (superior), the cover design?_____

4. On a scale from 1 (poor) to 10 (superior), please rate the following elements.

   _____ Heroine   _____ Plot

   _____ Hero   _____ Inspirational theme

   _____ Setting   _____ Secondary characters

5. These characters were special because_____
   _____
   _____

6. How has this book inspired your life?_____
   _____
   _____

7. What settings would you like to see covered in future
   Heartsong Presents books?_____
   _____
   _____

8. What are some inspirational themes you would like to see
   treated in future books?_____
   _____
   _____

9. Would you be interested in reading other **Heartsong
   Presents** titles?   Yes ☐   No ☐

10. Please check your age range:
    ☐ Under 18   ☐ 18-24   ☐ 25-34
    ☐ 35-45   ☐ 46-55   ☐ Over 55

11. How many hours per week do you read?_____

Name _____

Occupation _____

Address _____

City _____ State _____ Zip _____